Please return this book on or before the date shown above. To
renew go to www.essex.gov.uk/libraries, ring 0845 603 7628 or
go to any Essex library.

Essex County Council

'You did well, Meg. You probably saved that boy's life.'

'Well, I don't paint my nails or bake cookies, but I have some skills.' But maybe her skills weren't enough in this case. Suddenly she wanted to lean against that broad chest and just sob. She didn't care that she'd been resisting his advances for months. She just wanted to feel those strong arms close around her. 'Dino—'

'It's a good job I am here, no? A weak, feeble girl like you is going to need a big strong guy like me to help you out of this mess.'

Her traitorous desire to lean on him vanished instantly. 'I don't need any help from you.'

'*Sì*, of course you need my help.' His mouth curved into a slow, sexy smile. 'It's just you, me, and this little private room. This isn't quite how I pictured our first night together, but I can be flexible. Do you have any mistletoe?'

'If I had any mistletoe all I'd do with it is force-feed you the berries—'

Without warning he leaned towards her, and for one breathless, heart-stopping moment she thought he was going to kiss her. His eyes glittered dark with sexual promise, and Meg felt something she'd never let herself feel. Then she came to her senses and gave him a hard shove.

'You said you weren't in the mood,' he purred. 'I was going to put you in the mood.'

Sarah Morgan is a British writer who regularly tops the bestseller lists with her lively stories for both Mills & Boon® Medical™ Romance and Modern™ Romance.

As a child Sarah dreamed of being a writer, and although she took a few interesting detours on the way she is now living that dream. With her writing career she has successfully combined business with pleasure, and she firmly believes that reading romance is one of the most satisfying and fat-free escapist pleasures available. Her stories are unashamedly optimistic, and she is always pleased when she receives letters from readers saying that her books have helped them through hard times.

RT Book Reviews has described her writing as 'action-packed and sexy', and she has been nominated twice for a Reviewer's Choice Award and shortlisted twice for the Romance Prize by the Romantic Novelists' Association.

Sarah lives near London with her husband and two children, who innocently provide an endless supply of authentic dialogue. When she isn't writing or nagging about homework Sarah enjoys music, movies, and any activity that takes her outdoors.

Recent titles by the same author:

Medical™ Romance
CHRISTMAS EVE: DOORSTEP DELIVERY
SNOWBOUND: MIRACLE MARRIAGE
THE GREEK BILLIONAIRE'S LOVE-CHILD
ITALIAN DOCTOR, SLEIGH-BELL BRIDE

**Sarah Morgan also writes for Modern™ Romance.
Her sexy heroes and feisty heroines
aren't to be missed!**

DR ZINETTI'S SNOWKISSED BRIDE

BY
SARAH MORGAN

First published in Great Britain 2010
by Mills & Boon,
an imprint of Harlequin (UK) Limited,
Large Print edition 2011
Eton House, 18-24 Paradise Road,
Richmond, Surrey TW9 1SR

© Sarah Morgan 2010

ISBN: 978 0 263 21734 6

Harlequin (UK) policy is to use papers that are
natural, renewable and recyclable products and made
from wood grown in sustainable forests. The logging
and manufacturing process conform to the legal
environmental regulations of the country of origin.

Printed and bound in Great Britain
by CPI Antony Rowe, Chippenham, Wiltshire

DR ZINETTI'S
SNOWKISSED
BRIDE

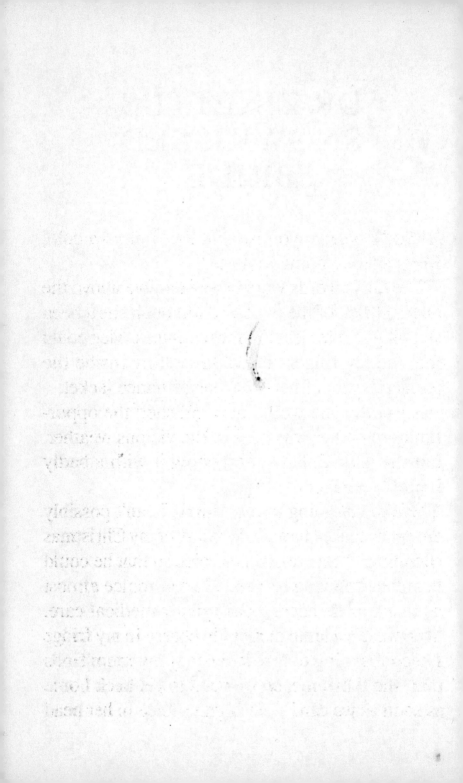

CHAPTER ONE

'I CAN'T believe you f-found me. I'm *s-so* cold, Meg. Are we going to d-die?'

The boy's words were barely audible above the angry shriek of the wind and although she'd been standing still for less than two minutes, Meg could feel the icy fingers of cold reaching inside the padded layers of her high-performance jacket.

Normally she would have relished the opportunity to pit her wits against the vicious weather, but she hadn't planned on doing it with a badly injured teenager.

'We're not going to die, Harry. I can't possibly die yet because I haven't done any of my Christmas shopping…' She raised her voice so that he could hear her, knowing he needed reassurance almost as much as he needed emergency medical care. 'And there's a lump of mouldy cheese in my fridge I keep meaning to throw away. If my mum finds that, she'll kill me, so we need to get back home as soon as we can.' Ignoring the voice in her head reminding her that the wind chill decreased the temperature to minus fifteen and that the teenager had nasty injuries, Meg tore open the top of her backpack and dragged out the equipment she needed. 'I've called the rest of the mountain rescue team. They're on their way. In the meantime, I'm going to get you out of this wind and keep you warm.' As if challenging that promise, the wind gave a furious howl and buffeted her body. She reached out and steadied herself with her gloved hand, putting her body between the wind and the boy.

Behind them were snow-covered layers of jagged rock and beneath them the side of the mountain fell away into a deep ravine where icy water formed a death trap, waiting to finish off what the rocks and the wind had started.

Meg pulled the collar of her jacket over her mouth and tried to catch her breath, ignoring the nagging worry that it was going to be impossible to evacuate him from this treacherous site with the wind so high.

Her priority had to be shelter. The rest could wait. If she didn't get him out of this biting wind in the next few minutes, there wouldn't be anyone alive to rescue.

She gave a whistle and Rambo, her German shepherd search-and-rescue dog, nosed his way over to the boy and sat in front of him, offering still more protection from the wind while Meg found what she needed.

'Right, Harry, prepare for luxury.' She shouted to make herself heard. 'What we need now is a nice, warm living room with a roaring log fire and a pretty Christmas tree, but this is the best I can do at short notice.' She flipped the portable tent she'd removed from her backpack and for a terrifying moment the wind caught it and almost pulled her off her feet. 'Oh, for… I need to eat more chocolate. I'm not heavy enough.' As she felt her feet lift off the snow, Meg yanked the fabric hard and managed to anchor it. Within seconds she and the injured boy were inside. 'Unfortunately no log fire and no Christmas tree,' she panted, brushing the snow away from her face, 'but this is better than nothing. All right, now I can look at you. What have you been doing to yourself, Harry? You look like an extra from a cheap horror movie.'

It was worse than she'd thought. In the fading light she could see the wicked gash on his head and the purple bruising spreading across his skin.

Harry lifted his bloodied hand to his head. 'Is it bad?'

'I've seen worse.'

'But you work in the emergency department, so that's not much comfort. You see people with half their bodies missing.'

'You're going to be fine, Harry.' Meg pulled off her glove and undid the straps of her backpack. 'You're going to have a bit of a headache tomorrow, but it's nothing that a few days in bed won't solve.' She kept her voice matter-of-fact, but she was listening to his responses, watching for any signs of confusion or disorientation as a result of the head injury. 'Were you knocked out?'

'I—I think so.'

'Do you know what day of the week it is?'

'Yes, it's Sunday,' he mumbled, 'and I'm going to be in a shit load of trouble for going out into the mountains.'

'Harry Baxter, you are not supposed to swear in public.'

He closed his eyes and leaned back against her backpack. 'Aren't you going to yell at me and ask me what I thought I was doing, coming up here on my own?'

Aware that hypothermia could kill him long before the head injury, Meg was busy covering him with extra layers. Another scarf. A coat. 'That's your mum's line, sweetheart. Rambo and I just do the rescuing. We leave the lecturing to others.'

At the mention of his mother, Harry's face went from white to grey. 'She's going to be worried sick. I told her I was only going out for an hour.'

'Yeah, well, that's part of being a mum. Goes with the territory.' Meg examined the wound on his head, took a photograph with her phone and then covered the injury with a sterile pad held in place with a bandage.

'Why are you taking photographs of me?'

'Because it will save the trauma team having to remove the dressing to see the wound. Just a precaution.' In case he needed to be taken straight to Theatre.

The tent flapped against her and Meg pushed back against the fabric, relieved they had at least some protection from the raging blizzard. They weren't exactly cosy, but at least they were out of the deadly wind. 'When you're a mum, you sign up for worry on a long-term basis. Someone on the MRT will have called her and told her we've found you. There's not much else I can do for your head, so I'm going to take a look at this arm of yours now. Tell me what happened when you fell. Can you remember?'

'I slipped on a patch of ice and fell over the edge of the gully. I remember falling and falling and then I smacked my head against a rock.' The boy opened his eyes and looked at her dizzily. 'When I woke up I had blood on my face and my wrist was a really funny shape. I could see the bone.'

Meg kept her expression neutral. 'Right. Well, that's something we're going to need to fix. You can't go around with a wrist that looks like that— you'll gross everyone out.'

His face was a strange shade, now somewhere between white and grey. He clutched her arm with his good hand. 'I thought I was going to die on my own here. I couldn't believe it when I heard Rambo barking. You're so cool, Meg. Dog-girl.'

Meg moved aside the extra layers and gently pulled up the sleeve of his jacket so that she could take a better look at his injuries. 'Harry, when you're a bit older you'll realise that calling a woman "dog-girl" isn't going to win you hearts.' There was an obvious fracture of the bone, his wrist shaped like a dinner fork. 'I don't mind "wolf-girl" but I draw the line at "dog-girl", if it's all the same to you.'

'That's what I meant. I know that's what the mountain rescue team call you because you and Rambo are such a good team. And you're so fit—not fit as in fit…' He coloured, backtracking wildly as he realised how his words could be construed. 'I mean fit in the sense that you run up the mountains without even getting out of breath, and…I…' His voice tailed off and his eyes drifted shut.

'Talk to me, Harry!' Meg felt a stab of alarm as she looked at the bruising on the side of his face. 'Tell me what you want for Christmas.' *Had he lost consciousness? Had he—?*

'At the moment?' He kept his eyes closed, as if it were too much effort to open them. 'Just to be lying in my bedroom. I have a funny feeling I'm never going to see it again.'

'You're going to see it.' Meg dug her hand into her backpack and pulled out the first-aid kit she always carried with her. 'Although if your room is anything like my Jamie's, I bet you can't see the floor anyway. What is it about boys and untidy rooms?'

'I can find everything in the mess. I like mess.' His voice was faint. 'Meg?'

'Right here, honey.'

'We're not going to make it, are we? No one is going to be able to get us down from here. Tell me honestly—I really want the truth. I'm thirteen now, not a kid.'

Still a kid, Meg thought, a lump in her throat. 'We're going to make it, Harry. I promise you that.' But it wasn't going to be easy. Looking at his badly injured wrist and the swelling on the side of his face, she felt her heart lurch. There was no way she was going to be able to walk him off this mountain. And he was right about the bone. It was sticking out. She took another photograph for the trauma team, quickly emailed it to her colleagues in the emergency department and then covered the wound with a sterile dressing and bandaged it in place. Outside the tent the wind howled and suddenly she felt horribly alone. What had started out as a relaxed training walk for her and Rambo had turned into a deadly storm and a seriously injured casualty at risk of hypothermia.

If she hadn't decided to walk today…

Pushing aside that thought, she pulled out a thermometer and checked his temperature. It was dropping and she'd used every layer she had. She was just wondering whether she could risk giving him her jacket when she heard Rambo bark.

Meg felt a rush of relief. 'He's telling me that reinforcements have arrived. That must be the mountain rescue team. You just hang in there for a few more minutes, Harry. We're going to get you something for the pain and then get you out of this ravine.'

Tucking the coat around him, she went on her hands and knees and poked her head out of her tent. Through the swirling snow she saw powerful male legs, and then a man squatted down to her level and she found herself staring into glittering dark eyes that made her heart flip.

'Well,' he drawled, 'if it isn't wolf-girl.'

Meg was so relieved to see him that for once she didn't react. 'Dino, thank God you're here! Where are the rest of the team?'

'Just me so far.' His voice calm, he swung his backpack off his back. 'But quality is always better than quantity. Except in my case, you get both.' He gave her a sexy wink. 'Relax. What you

need is a big, strong man and here I am so your
worries are over, *amore*. I will handle everything
now.'

Meg gave him a withering look. 'I'm not, and
never will be, your *amore*. And I don't need you
to handle anything. I can handle it myself. I've
been handling it while you've no doubt been out
to a fancy restaurant for Sunday lunch with some
skinny blonde.'

With a maddening smile, he pushed past her
into the tiny tent. 'She was brunette.'

'This tent isn't big enough for you and me,'
Meg gritted, but he ignored her, his leg brushing against hers as he settled himself next to the
injured boy. His wide shoulders pressed against
the flimsy tent and there was barely room left to
breathe, but that didn't seem to bother him. And,
for once, it didn't bother her either. Not that she
would ever have admitted it, but she was really
relieved it was him.

Dino Zinetti might be too good looking for his
own good, he might drive her crazy and make
her feel horribly uncomfortable, but he was also a
skilled doctor and an experienced mountaineer.

'You chose lovely weather for your trip, Harry.'
He sat next to the injured boy, the same eyes that

had been seducing her moments earlier now sharp and focused, the sexy smile replaced with a reassuring one. 'You seem to have got yourself in a spot of bother. You're lucky wolf-girl happened to be out today on one of her lone walks.'

Harry's lips were turning blue. 'I made a mistake. I called her dog-girl.'

'Ah…' Dino's eyes crinkled at the corners. 'In a couple more years I'll give you some tips on the right and wrong things to say to women.' His tone was relaxed and easy, in direct contrast to his fingers, which were working swiftly, checking pulse, pupils and other signs. 'Do you know if you knocked yourself out?' He questioned the boy, interspersing reassurance with questions designed to aid his clinical judgement.

'He might have done. GCS of fifteen when I got here but that's a nasty gash on his head. I think he needs a CT scan. Do you reckon the helicopter might still make it, or is the weather too bad?' Cramped in the confines of the tiny tent, Meg found it unsettling to be pressed so close to him. 'Are we going to have to wait it out for a few hours?'

'You want to leave this place?' Smiling, Dino checked Harry's pupils, asked him another couple of questions and then turned his attention to the broken wrist. 'Are you telling me this isn't the most romantic place you've ever spent a night? A beautiful woman, alone with two strong men?'

'One strong man. I don't think I count.' Harry gave a weak smile. 'You're pretty smooth, Dr Zinetti. When I'm older, I want to be like you.'

'Trust me, you don't.' Meg squashed herself against the tent to make as much space as possible. 'Not unless you want to walk around with a permanent black eye courtesy of all the women who have punched you. Dr Zinetti is Italian so that's how he gets away with being so politically incorrect. You don't have that excuse. And you do count, Harry.'

'I don't think so. I don't feel too good…' Harry's eyes drifted closed and this time didn't open again.

Meg felt her heart do an emergency stop. Instead of focusing on not allowing any of her body parts to touch Dino, she concentrated on Harry. 'He—'

'Take a breath, wolf-girl,' Dino said calmly. 'There's a spare jacket in my backpack and a space blanket. Get them both on him because his temperature is dropping and I don't want to add hypothermia to his list of problems. Time to call in the cavalry.' He reached into his pocket and pulled out a satellite phone while Meg tucked the extra insulation around the injured boy.

As Dino talked to the search-and-rescue team, giving GPS co-ordinates, she was thinking about how worried Harry's mother would be.

'They're going to scramble a helicopter.' Dino rocked back on his heels, frowning as the tent flapped against his back. 'I think he needs a faster trip to hospital than we can give him on a stretcher.'

'The wind is too high for the helicopter.'

'It's dropped slightly. They're going to give it a try, although of course it won't be easy given that we're in a gully.' He gave a humourless smile. 'Let's hope the winchman likes a challenge. Is Rambo all right with noisy helicopters?'

'Of course. He's flown in them more times than you.' Meg was looking at Harry, worried about his pallor. 'Dino—'

'I know. I see. I agree with you that we need to get him to hospital and do a CT scan. I've rung the department.'

'Who is on duty this evening?'

'Sean Nicholson. And the helicopter crew

picked up Daniel Buchannan when they received our call.'

In the confines of the tent, their faces were close. She could see the thickness of his eyelashes and the beginnings of stubble on his jaw. It was a face so handsome that no woman passed him without taking a long, covetous look. Except her. Resolutely, she looked the other way. The day she started noticing that he was handsome was the day she was in trouble. So he had sexy eyes. *So what?* 'So you're not going in the helicopter?'

'No. I'm staying with you, wolf-girl.' Suddenly those sexy eyes were deadly serious. 'What were you doing up here, Meg? Hardly the weather for an evening stroll. Blizzard, drifting snow, wind chill…'

'Perfect evening for a walk.' Meg didn't bother telling him that was how she liked the weather. Wild and crazy. She'd given up explaining herself to people years before. 'Anyway, you should be thanking me. If I hadn't decided to walk, I wouldn't have found Harry. I didn't plan to come up this far but Rambo picked up the scent.'

'You should be at home, baking cookies or painting your nails.'

Even though she knew he was intentionally

trying to wind her up she was still shocked by the emotion that rushed through her body. Why did comments like that still bother her so much? Reminding herself that it had been nothing more than a flippant remark on his part, Meg pulled a face. 'I'd rather be blown off a ridge in a force-nine gale than paint my nails. *Not* that I expect you to understand that. The women you date can't walk and blink at the same time. The one today—could she talk and eat her lunch?'

'Jealous, *amore*?'

'No. I'd rather poke myself in the eye with a fork than have a romantic lunch with you.'

'Is that so? You have strange aspirations, Meg Miller.' Humour in his eyes, Dino watched her for a moment and then turned back to Harry, checking his temperature and other vital signs again. 'His GCS is dropping.'

'Perhaps we should—' Meg broke off as Dino put a hand on her arm.

'Listen. No wind. Must be the eye of the storm.'

All she could hear was the throb of blood in her ears. She told herself it had absolutely nothing to do with the touch of his hand on her arm and the fact that they couldn't move without brushing past each other. Forcing herself to focus, she realised that the tent was no longer flapping so violently. 'I can hear the helicopter.' She stuck her head out of the opening and saw lights approaching high above them. 'They'll have to hover above the gully.'

'I'll make sure everything is strapped down.' Dino crawled out of the tent to help the helicopter crew and Meg's gaze lingered on his shoulders. She was an athlete, she told herself. It was natural that she'd admire honed muscle and a powerful physique.

He stood on the narrow, snow-covered path, ready to assist the winchman. As the helicopter hovered above the narrow gully, the downdraft caused the sides of the tent to flap and whip up the new snow. Given the potential hazards, there was no wasted time. The winchman was lowered out of the helicopter and together the three of them strapped Harry securely to the stretcher, protecting his back and his neck. As he was winched back up into the helicopter, Dino held the guide rope to help prevent the potentially lethal swing of the winch rope into the sides of the gully. Once Harry was safely inside the helicopter, the crew released the guide rope and disappeared into the darkness.

Meg felt the adrenaline drain away and relief take its place. It was almost weakness, this response after the event, and she slid back inside the tent and sat for a moment, breathing slowly, trying not to think of all the alternative scenarios that tried to destabilise her sense of calm.

What if she hadn't found him?

What if Dino hadn't come?

She covered her face with her hands, dimly aware that Dino had gathered up the guide rope and was now back in the tent with her. 'I've known Harry since he was born. My mum knows his mum. I used to go round and help bath him when I was a kid.'

'Lucky Harry.' Dino stowed the guide rope in his backpack and then gently removed her hands from her face. 'You did well, wolf-girl. You probably saved his life.'

'Well, I don't paint my nails or bake cookies, but I have some skills.' But maybe her skills weren't enough in this case. What if he had a depressed skull fracture? What if they didn't get him to hospital fast enough? Now that the immediate crisis was over, the fear that had been pressing against her threatened to overwhelm her. Suddenly she wanted to lean against that broad chest and just sob. She didn't care that he was a notorious heart-breaker and that she'd been resisting his advances for months. She just wanted to feel those strong arms close around her. 'Dino—'

'It's a good job I am here, no? A weak, feeble girl like you is going to need a big strong guy like me to help you out of this mess.'

Her traitorous desire to lean on him vanished instantly. 'Do you honestly think I need your help?' Anger stoked the fire inside her that had burned down to no more than a few glowing embers. 'I don't need any help from you.'

'*Sì*, of course you need my help.' He started piling the equipment back inside his bag. 'You are too small and delicate to walk down this mountain without assistance. The wind has dropped, but not for long. You wouldn't be fit enough to walk as fast as you'd need to. We will stay the night here, and I will protect you.' His mouth curved into a slow, sexy smile. 'It's just you, me and this little private room. This isn't quite how I pictured our first night together, but I can be flexible. Do you have any mistletoe?'

Anger flushed away the worry about Harry. 'If

I had any mistletoe all I'd do with it is force-feed you the berries. I'm not in the mood, Dino—'

Without warning, he leaned towards her and for one breathless, heart-stopping moment she thought he was going to kiss her. His eyes glittered dark with sexual promise and Meg felt something she never let herself feel. She felt strangely disconnected, as if she were being controlled by some invisible force outside herself. Then she came to her senses and gave him a hard shove.

'What the hell do you think you're doing?'

'You said you weren't in the mood,' he purred. 'I was going to put you in the mood.'

'I meant that I wasn't in the mood for your flirting,' she croaked, 'not—anything else.' It was disconcerting to realise that her hands were shaking. She knew that if she'd been standing up, her knees would have been shaking, too.

'That's what you meant?' Those sexy eyes teased her. 'Then you need to be more specific when you communicate.'

Her lips were tingling and the blood was rushing around her body. 'Don't *ever* do that again, Zinetti!'

'Do what?' Dino smiled and trailed a finger over her cheek. 'I haven't done anything yet.

Maybe this is a good moment to teach you all the practical applications of the use of body warmth in the prevention of hypothermia.'

Meg skidded to the furthest point of the tent, too aggravated by her own response to notice his brief, satisfied smile. 'I wouldn't spend a night cosied up with you if we were the only two people left on the planet. I'd rather *die* of hypothermia.'

'Beautiful Megan.' His voice was soft. 'A woman like you should have a man in her life, but you do everything alone.'

'That's the way I like it.'

'Because you are afraid?'

It was like dropping a lighted match into a haystack. 'Dino.' Meg hauled the anger back inside herself. 'You're the one who should be afraid. Get out of my tent. I want to go down, now. I can't stand another five minutes stuck on this rock face with a smooth-talking Italian. You're more lethal than the weather.'

To her surprise he didn't argue with her. Instead, he helped her pack up the equipment with his usual ruthless efficiency and then switched on the headlamp on his helmet.

Meg was so furious, so tumbled up inside that

she barely noticed the steep descent. Dino stayed a metre in front of her all the way down, which gave her plenty of time to glare at his shoulders and plan various methods of revenge. Maybe she'd do something really embarrassing when he was surrounded by a bunch of nurse groupies. Maybe she'd even give him that kiss he'd been teasing her with. She could fry his brain and teach him a lesson. Just because she didn't paint her nails, it didn't mean she didn't know how to kiss, did it?

They trudged and stumbled through the deep snow and the inky darkness until they reached low ground and all the time Rambo panted alongside her, his shape a reassuring presence in the vicious weather.

It was only as they were striding across the safety of the valley floor that the adrenaline ceased to pump round her body and her brain started to work properly. And then she realised what Dino had done.

She stopped for a moment, cursing herself for being dense and slow.

Dino turned with a frown. 'Not a good place to stop, wolf-girl. Something wrong?'

'You did that on purpose, didn't you?' The wind

gusted, almost blowing her over. 'You made me angry, you—'

With a maddening smile, Dino shrugged and carried on walking.

Meg glared after him, feeling like a fool. He hadn't wanted to kiss her. It had just been a ploy to stop her worrying about Harry. She strode after him and caught up with him at the car. 'There are times when you really drive me mad, Dr Zinetti.'

'I rely on it. Need any help with that backpack?' He slid his own off his back and threw it into the boot.

'I can handle my own backpack.' She spat the words. 'And I can handle myself up a mountain. I don't need you—' She almost said 'messing with my head' but just in time she decided that she didn't want him to know that the thought of kissing him filled her with anything other than feelings of boredom.

'You were going to cry, wolf-girl, and I didn't want a hysterical woman on the mountain with me. I'd rather deal with ten fractured skulls than one hysterical woman.'

'I was *not* hysterical and I was *not* going to cry.'

'You were getting really wobbly and there's no way I could have got you down this mountain in that feeble state.'

'*Feeble!*' Meg took a breath as the extent of his manipulation sank in. 'You never intended us to spend the night on the mountain—'

'I enjoy extreme mountain survival as much as the next macho guy...' he closed the boot '...but I was worried about you. You don't exactly carry much body fat. Keeping warm would have been a challenge. Talking of which, we need to get out of this wind.'

He'd goaded her and then he'd almost—and she'd almost—'I hate you.'

'No you don't.' He placed an arm on either side of her so that her back was pressed against the car, with no opportunity to escape. 'You're afraid of what you feel for me, *amore*, and that's understandable because it's very powerful.' He dragged his gloved hand over her cheek, a thoughtful look on his face. 'Interesting, isn't it? Wolf-girl, who never lets a man near her, suddenly feeling the chemistry.'

For a moment, Meg was transfixed by those night-black eyes. 'No, it isn't interesting. The last thing I need in my life is a Mediterranean macho man. You're not my type and I'm certainly not yours.'

'You don't know me well enough to make that judgement.'

'Maybe I don't want to know you.' She shoved at his chest but he didn't budge. 'Dino…'

Rambo growled low in his throat and Dino smiled and released her.

'I have more sense than to come between wolf-girl and her wolf.' He spoke quietly to Rambo in Italian and Meg felt her stomach flip because, although she wouldn't have admitted it in a million years, the words sounded so lyrical and sexy.

'He's protecting me.'

'I know. He's an excellent dog. But you don't need to be protected from me. I'm not the enemy.' Not remotely afraid of the dog, Dino stroked Rambo's head gently. 'He's never growled at me before.'

'You've never pinned me to the car before.' She tried not to show how flustered she felt. It was as if his powerful body had imprinted against hers. Even though he'd moved she could still feel it, hard and heavy. 'He growled at you because I pushed you and you didn't move. He was giving you a warning. Which makes two of us.'

'Will he let you give me a lift? I left my Lamborghini outside your cottage.'

'You drove the Lamborghini in this weather?' Meg glanced at the ice and snow covering the road and then back at him in disbelief. There was a devilish gleam in his eyes and his face was breathtakingly handsome in the moonlight. 'The roads are lethal.'

'Like you, I love a challenge.'

And that was why he was dangerous. Like her, he loved the adrenaline rush. 'I'm tempted to let you walk from here to the brunette who is probably waiting for you at home. The cold air will do you good.'

'No one is waiting for me at home, Meg. And I'm going to the hospital. They're overstretched and I want to check on Harry.'

Feeling really stupid, Meg let out an exasperated breath. 'You see? It's things like that I find really infuriating! Just when I'm ready to dismiss you as shallow you do something really—really…' She floundered and then shrugged. 'Decent. Go on. Get in before I change my mind. Rambo, don't eat him. He's going to help Harry. That's the only reason we're letting him live.'

Trying not to think about the moment when

he'd almost kissed her, she drove her four-wheel drive down the narrow roads that led towards her cottage. 'I can't believe you drove the Lamborghini.'

'I was at lunch, remember? With a woman.'

'So the Lamborghini is an essential part of the Zinetti seduction technique?' For some reason it irritated her and she changed gears viciously. 'Do some women really fall for that?'

'All of them. Could you slow down before you kill us both?'

'I've driven these roads since I was a teenager. You must mix with some shallow women.'

'I do my best. You drive too fast, Meg.'

'Coming from someone who owns a Lamborghini *and* a Ferrari, that's a bit rich. Don't tell me—you're such a chauvinist you hate being driven by a woman.'

Dino's fingers were gripping the seat. 'I hate being driven by anyone.'

'That's because you're a control freak.'

'*Sì*, I admit that. I like being the one in charge.' He glanced towards her, laughter in his eyes. 'I like to be the one on top, so to speak.'

'Well, that confirms I'm not your type, because I like to be the one on top, too.' Meg increased her speed, taking pleasure from his sudden indrawn breath. 'Two control freaks together is a recipe for disaster.'

'Or a recipe for explosive passion. Shall we find out which it is?'

Just for a moment her concentration lapsed and she felt the wheels of her four-by-four lose traction as she hit ice. She resisted the impulse to hit the brakes and steered into the skid, regaining control of the car within seconds. 'That was fun.' Her heart was pounding and her mouth was dry. 'At least it shut you up. Are you all right?'

'You mean apart from my heart attack?' His sardonic drawl made her smile and she slowed her speed.

'Why did you leave your car outside my house?'

'When Harry's mother realised he was missing, she called the team. Then she called your mother because she remembered that the gully is a favourite walk of yours and Harry often watches you and Rambo training up there. She hoped you might already be out, which you were. I dropped by to get your route from your mother.'

Meg tightened her grip on the wheel. 'So this is all my fault because he followed me?'

'No. It's Harry's fault. He went for a walk in the winter without the right equipment.'

'He was unlucky.'

'No, he was lucky.' Dino pulled off a glove and flexed his fingers. 'You found him. Could have been worse.'

She was concentrating on the road but she could feel him looking at her. 'It was Rambo who picked up the scent. I didn't even know he was missing.'

'We were about to call you when you called us.'

'So how come you got to us so quickly and the others didn't?'

'I was about to head into the mountains myself. I guess we spend our free time the same way.'

'So your date didn't end the way you wanted it to.'

He smiled. 'It ended exactly the way I wanted it to.'

Which meant what, exactly? He'd already said the brunette wasn't waiting for him at home. Trying not to think about it, Meg pulled up outside her cottage. 'Home, sweet home. And you're still in one piece.'

'Miracles do happen. Thanks for the lift. Are you working tomorrow?'

'Yes. Look, Dino…' She hesitated, torn between getting away from him as fast as possible and doing the right thing for Harry. 'Don't take the Lamborghini. We've had so much snow in the past few hours and your car isn't good in bad weather. I'll drive you to the hospital. If they're as busy as you say, they could probably use my help as well as yours. Just give me time to explain to Mum and see Jamie.'

Meg slid out of the car and crunched her way through layers of snow to the front door of her cottage. She stood for a moment, looking at the lights burning in the windows and the rose bush groaning under the weight of snow by the front door. In a few more months it would be frothy with white blooms, turning her home into something from a picture postcard. The summer tourists who overran the Lake District like a million invading ants had been known to stop and take photographs of her house because it was so quintessentially English. To her it was home and she loved it. Now, with Christmas only two weeks away, there was a wreath on the door and scarlet berries on the holly bush. And mistletoe.

Meg frowned.

Who had added the mistletoe?

The door opened before she even started to delve for her key and her mother stood there, an apron tied round her slim waist, a mug in her hand. 'I've made you hot soup, Dr Zinetti. You need something to warm you before you go back to the hospital.'

'*Molto grazie*. You are truly a life saver, Mrs Miller.' Dino emerged from behind her and took the mug in his gloved hand, the steam from the soup forming clouds in the freezing air. 'I'm grateful.'

'I'm the one who is grateful. You brought my girl safely home.'

'I brought myself home, Mum. Do I get soup, too?' Irritated, Meg dragged the hat off her head and immediately saw Dino's expression change as he followed the crazy tumble of her hair with narrowed eyes.

She tensed, thinking that he was probably comparing her messy, tangled hair to the smooth, blow-dried version he'd stared at across the lunch table a few hours earlier. For a moment she wished she'd left her hat on and that thought annoyed her because she'd long ago come to terms with who she was. When other girls in her school had been learning about lipstick and moisturiser, she'd been learning to map read and use a compass. While they'd spent their weekends shopping for clothes, she'd been up on the mountains. Her only interest in clothes was whether they were wind resistant and weatherproof. She knew about wicking layers and the importance of not wearing cotton. She didn't know whether grey was the new black or whether jeans should be straight cut or boot cut. And, more to the point, she didn't care.

Meg turned away, irritated with him for looking and even more irritated with herself for caring that he'd looked.

What could have been a decidedly awkward moment was broken by her mother's disapproving tone.

'Megan, I found mouldy cheese in your fridge.'

Meg gritted her teeth and vowed never to let her mother babysit again. 'Is Jamie still awake?'

'Mummy?' Right on cue a small figure dressed in a Batman costume barrelled into her, crushing her round the waist. 'We decorated the house. We've put mistletoe everywhere.'

'I'd noticed.' Why was everyone suddenly so obsessed with mistletoe?

'Grandma says the berries are magic. If you stand under them, exciting things can happen.'

'Is that right?' Meg dropped to her knees and hugged her son. Immediately she felt her mood soften and the tension in her limbs evaporate. He smelled of shampoo and bedtime and his smile was the best thing she'd seen all day.

As long as she had him, everything was all right with her world.

'Hey there, Batman.' Dino was smiling. 'Have you saved Gotham City lately?'

'Loads of times.' Jamie wrapped his arms round Meg's neck, shivering in the thin costume he insisted on wearing to bed but grinning up at Dino anyway. For some reason that Meg didn't even want to think about, in the months that she'd been working alongside Dino, her son had developed a serious case of hero-worship for him. 'Why? Do you need any help?'

'When I do, you'll be the first person I ask. I need to get back to the hospital.' Dino retrieved his car keys from his pocket.

'Did you drive the Lamborghini? Wow, that's

so cool. It looks like the Batmobile. Can I sit in it?'

Meg tensed. 'No, Jamie, you—'

'Just for a minute—pleeease?'

Anticipating Dino's inevitable rejection and Jamie's subsequent disappointment, Meg shook her head. 'Dino has to go, Jamie. He's a very important doctor and he's needed at the hospital. And, anyway, I know you love cars but the temperature is minus five and you're in your Batman costume. You need to get back inside.'

'Batman doesn't feel the cold.'

'You heard Dr Zinetti, he has to get back to the hospital now. Another time, perhaps.' Having made his excuses for him, she expected Dino to leave, but instead he handed his empty mug back to her mother.

'Does Batman have a cloak or some sort of coat? Anything you could wear over your outfit?'

Jamie frowned. 'I'm not cold. Batman is tough and strong.'

'I know,' Dino didn't miss a beat. 'But the neighbours might be watching and you don't want them to know who you really are. A superhero likes to keep his identity a secret.'

Jamie turned his head and looked at the

neighbouring cottages. 'You think they might be watching?'

'I think you can't be too careful when you're saving the world.' Dino's expression was serious. 'If you have something warm that will cover up who you are, we could sit in the Batmobile for a few minutes and discuss tactics.'

'Really?' Jamie's face lit up like the lights on a Christmas tree. 'Wait there.' He sped into the house and returned moments later in his warm ski jacket, trainers on his bare feet. In his hand was a plastic Batman figure. Seeing the excitement in his face, Meg frowned.

'Jamie, you can't—'

Ignoring her, he hurled himself at Dino, who caught him with a laugh, swung him round and then lifted him onto his shoulders and carried him to the car.

Gripped by a fear that she couldn't control, Meg watched as cracks appeared in her tightly controlled life. Jamie's delighted giggles cut through the night air and she plunged her hands into the pockets of her coat, resisting the temptation to snatch him back. *Keep him from harm.*

'Dino is good with him.' Her mother handed her a mug of soup. 'I can't believe he's actually managed to get Jamie to wear a coat. It's more than I've been able to do all day. This is worse than the Tarzan phase when he ran around in nothing but his underpants for two whole months.'

Meg found it difficult to move her lips. As much as it pained her to admit it, she agreed—Dino was brilliant with Jamie, and that was a whole big problem in itself. 'Yes.'

'It's a pleasant change for Jamie to have a man about the place. They look good together, don't they? Doesn't it warm your heart to see it?'

'No, actually.' Meg had never felt colder in her life. 'It just reminds me how little Jamie knows about the real world.' How easy it was to be hurt. *The more you gave, the more you could lose.*

'Chill, Megan.'

Meg turned her head to look at her mother. 'Since when did you start speaking like a teenager?'

'Since I started working at the youth group,' her mother said cheerfully. 'I love it. They're so vibrant and full of hope. Gives me something to do when I'm not helping you with Jamie. Oh, look at Jamie jumping in the seat! He's enjoying himself, Meg. He likes Dino. And Dino likes him.'

'Yes, because it suits him right now. And will

until the next female distraction walks across his path and he has someone better to play with than my son. What then?' Meg's tone was savage. Her worries suddenly overflowed, like a river bursting its banks. 'Presumably I'm the one who is going to have to explain to Jamie why Dino doesn't have time for him any more. I'm going to have to break it to him that men often have a short attention span.' She shivered as Dino fired up the engine, indulging her son's passion for supercars. The Lamborghini gave a deep, throaty growl and Jamie bounced around in the passenger seat in paroxysms of delight.

Aware that her mother was staring at her in astonishment, Meg licked her lips. 'Sorry,' she croaked, 'I'm tired. Maybe that was a bit of an overreaction.'

'Just a bit? Megan, you're a basket case when it comes to men.'

'I know.'

'Just because Hayden couldn't keep his trousers zipped, it doesn't mean all men are the same. You need to move on, Megan.'

'I've moved on. I'm living a good life with my child.' Huddling down inside her coat, Meg watched as Dino switched off the engine and let

Jamie play with the wheel for a few minutes, pretending to be a racing driver. 'Why does Jamie have to be interested in cars? It's the one thing I know absolutely nothing about.'

'He's a little boy.' Her mother's face softened. 'A gorgeous, fantastic boy and you have to help him grow into a gorgeous, fantastic man. That's your job. Part of that is letting him mix with men.'

'He does mix with men.'

'I'm not talking about the mountain rescue team. They treat you as one of the lads. I'm talking about man-woman stuff. He needs to see men as part of your life. When did you last go on a date?'

'You know I don't go on dates.' She blew on her hands to warm them. 'And there's no way I'm introducing a string of men to Jamie. What happens when they dump me? Jamie gets hurt. No way.'

'Maybe they wouldn't dump you. Have you thought about that?'

Meg stared straight ahead, her breath forming clouds in the freezing air. Her brain fielded the memories that came rushing forward to swamp her. 'My job is to protect my child. That's what mothers are supposed to do.'

'Are you protecting him? Or are you protecting yourself?' Her mother's voice was casual. 'Talking about protecting yourself, it's lucky Dino was able to find you and help you out on the mountain today.'

'I didn't need his help. I could have managed on my own.'

'Megan, when are you going to realise that you don't win awards in this life for managing on your own?' Her mother looked tired suddenly. 'You're a fantastic mum, but Jamie needs a man in his life and, frankly, so do you. It's time you stopped shutting everyone out. If you can't bring yourself to trust another man quite yet, at least make a New Year's resolution to have sex.'

'*Sex?*' Scandalised, Meg shrieked the word just as Dino scooped Jamie out of the car.

It echoed through the silence, the sound somehow magnified by the cold emptiness of the night.

Across the snow Dino's eyes met hers.

And she knew she was in trouble.

CHAPTER TWO

'MUMMY, what's sex?'

Oh, brilliant. Cursing her mother for landing her in such deep water, Meg tucked the duvet around Jamie. 'Well, sex can mean different things.' This was one conversation she did *not* want to have right now—not while memories of Dino's irresistible dark eyes were still fixed in her brain. 'It can mean the same thing as gender—whether someone is male or female.'

'So Rambo is male sex.'

'That's right.'

'And you're female sex.'

'Right again.'

Jamie reached for his drink of water. 'So what else does it mean?'

Meg wondered whether to simply change the subject and then decided that wouldn't be right. This was part of being a single parent, wasn't it? You dealt with these things on your own. 'When a male and a female come together to make a baby, that's called sex, too.' She decided that was enough detail for a seven-year-old, at least for the time being.

'Grandma thinks you should make a baby.'

Meg gulped. 'No, Jamie, that's not what Grandma thinks.'

'Yes, she does. She's told me loads of times she thinks you should get married and have more babies. She's always talking about it.'

Meg contemplated calling her mother upstairs to sort out the mess she'd created. 'Jamie, I'm not getting married.' She took the cup from him and tucked the duvet around him. 'Honestly, if I ever decide to get married, you'll be the first to know.'

'The man you're marrying would be the first to know. I'd be second.'

'Sometimes, my little superhero, you're too clever for your own good.' Meg kissed him on the cheek and then reached across and snapped the light on by his bed. 'Which story do you want?'

'Batman. So if you're not getting married, why did you yell the word "sex"? And why was Dino laughing so hard?' Jamie snuggled under the duvet, his hair still rumpled from play-fighting with the Italian doctor. His Batman toy was still in his hand. 'I don't get what's funny.'

'Nothing's funny. I was talking to Grandma. She was being…well, she was being Grandma.'

'She also told me it isn't normal or natural for a young woman of your age to be on her own,' Jamie parroted. 'I pointed out I live here too, but apparently I don't count.'

'You count, Jamie.' Meg picked up the book they'd been reading the night before. 'Believe me, you count.'

'I wouldn't mind if you got married. Especially if you married Dino. That would be super-cool.'

Meg thought about the heat they'd generated in the small tent on the mountainside. 'Cool' wasn't the word she would have chosen. 'Jamie, I'm not marrying Dino. We're not even…well…'

'You're not dating?'

'What do you know about dating?'

'It's when a boy and a girl hold hands. Sometimes they kiss and stuff. I know you don't do it.'

'Right. Well, that's because I haven't met anyone I want to…' she cleared her throat '…hold hands with.'

'Maybe you will now we've hung all the mistletoe

everywhere. Grandma says you just won't let a man close enough to hold your hand.'

'Grandma talks too much.'

'But it could happen?'

Not in a million years. 'Maybe—of course, you never know what will happen in this world.'

'Could it happen by Thursday?'

'Thursday?' Meg blinked. 'Why Thursday?'

'Thursday is Dad's Day at school.' He sounded gloomy. 'You're supposed to bring in your dad or some other important man in your life and they're all meant to talk about their jobs for five minutes.'

Meg felt as though ice water had been poured down her back. 'There are lots of kids in your school whose parents have split up.'

'Not in my class. Only Kevin and he still sees his dad every weekend. I'm the only one whose dad doesn't actually visit. Freddie King says I must be a total loser if even my own dad doesn't want to be with me.' Jamie sat up and scrubbed his hand over his face. 'I know you told me to be ass-ass—'

'Assertive.'

'That's what I meant—assertive, but it's hard

to be assertive when he's telling the truth.' His little mouth wobbled.

'It isn't the truth, Jamie.' Meg felt boiling-hot anger replace the freezing cold. 'Dad didn't leave because of you,' she muttered thickly, pulling him into her arms and hugging him tightly. The plastic Batman dug into her back. 'He left because of me. I've told you that a thousand times. He left before you were even born, so how could it have been about you? Technically, you weren't even here.'

'The thought of me was enough to scare him away.'

'It wasn't you who scared him away, it was me. I wasn't who he wanted me to be.' Meg eased him away from her. 'Your dad wanted a really girly girl, and I'm, well, I'm not like that. I've never been that great with hair and dresses and make-up and all that stuff.'

But other women were.

Do you really need to ask why I had an affair with Georgina? Because she's glamorous, Meg, that's why.

Meg sat still, shocked by how much it could still hurt, even after more than seven years.

Jamie snuggled under the covers, clearly

reassured by her words. 'But you can do all the important things. You're like Mrs Incredible. I mean, not with the stretchy arms, but you can climb, and slide down ropes and stuff. That's cool.'

Mrs Incredible. Meg swallowed down the lump in her throat. 'Well, *you* think it's cool, but some people think it's more important to know about the right shade of nail varnish than be able to rescue someone off a mountain in a blizzard.' She stroked his head quickly and then stood up, too agitated to sit still a moment longer. She prowled around the tiny bedroom, picking up socks and more Batman toys, trying not to remember how hard she'd found it to fit in at school. She didn't want her child to go through the same thing. She didn't want him to feel that same sense of isolation. 'It's going to be OK, Jamie. Tomorrow I'm going to talk to your teacher and ask her what on earth she was thinking, having Dad's Day at school. It just makes kids a target for bullying. We'll sort it out, I promise. We'll come up with a plan.'

Jamie was silent for a moment. 'I sort of had a plan. I thought of something.'

'Good. That's what I like. A plan. It's great that you sort things out by yourself. Tell me.'

'I want to invite Dino.'

Meg froze. 'To Dad's Day?'

'Why not? He lets me ride in his car, he's always nice to me when we have to go the mountain rescue centre and that time at the hospital he let me wait in his office and got me a whole bunch of toys to play with. And he knows about cars and stuff. I like him. He's nice.'

Nice? Meg thought about Dino Zinetti. Hair as dark as night, a mouth that was masculine and sexy and eyes that knew just how to look at a woman.

'Nice isn't the word I'd use.'

Jamie looked shocked. 'You don't think Dino is nice?'

'I'm not saying he isn't nice, honey.' 'Nice' seemed like such an inappropriate word to describe a man as hotly sexual as Dino, but somehow Meg managed to get her tongue round it. 'He is—er—nice, but, well…he's just not the right person to take to Dad's Day.'

'It doesn't have to be your dad. Just a man who is important in your life.'

And she didn't let Jamie have a man who was

important in his life, did she? This was all her fault. Torn apart by guilt, Meg stood still. 'Jamie, listen, I—'

'You work with him every day. Will you ask him, Mum? He just has to come for an hour and chat about what he does.'

Ask Dino to come to the school? Meg felt the Batman toy bite into her palm as she squeezed it tight. 'He wouldn't do that.'

'He might. You didn't think he'd let me sit in his car, and he did. You don't know if you don't ask.'

'I can't ask, Jamie.'

Jamie's face fell. 'OK. I'll just go on my own. It'll be fine.'

Meg felt like the worst mother in the world. 'All right, I'll ask him.' The words were torn from her, dragged from inside her by the raw power of maternal guilt. 'But he might be busy.'

'I know. He's a consultant in Emergency Medicine and he's a member of the mountain rescue team *and* he won a gold medal in the men's downhill at the winter Olympics when he was nineteen.'

'I beg your pardon?'

'He won a gold medal. Didn't you know?'

'No,' Meg said faintly. 'I didn't. We don't talk about personal stuff that much.'

'You should. He's really cool, Mum. Did you know that when he was my age he could eat six doughnuts in under a minute?'

Meg thought of Dino's athletic physique, a result of his active, outdoor lifestyle. 'No, I didn't know that either. Presumably he gave that habit up before he won the men's downhill. Go to sleep now.' Why on earth had she allowed herself to say she would speak to Dino? She'd rather dig a hole and bury herself in it. 'Jamie, listen to me—'

'I'm so glad you're going to ask him, Mum.' Jamie pulled the duvet up to his neck, a blissful smile on his face. 'I was dreading school this week, but now I'm really looking forward to it. Dino's the best. If he comes and talks to my class, Freddie will never tease me again. Do you know it's only fifteen more sleeps until Christmas? Isn't that great? I've written my letter to Santa. I did it with Grandma. We put it in the fireplace. Do you think he'll take it tonight?'

Meg opened her mouth to tell him that there was no way she could ask Dino to Dad's Day. 'I'm sure Santa will take it. Is it really only fifteen more sleeps?' Her voice was croaky and somehow she just couldn't form the right words. 'That is great. I guess I'd better start doing some Christmas shopping.'

Hi, Dino, what are you doing on Thursday?

Hi, Dino, don't take this the wrong way, but would you consider…?

Meg rehearsed various ways of asking him as she walked through the main entrance of the hospital the following morning. As if she didn't have enough pressure from her mother, now she had it from her son, too.

Why did she have to find a man? It was just nonsense. Jamie's life was full of men. Just not one special man. And that was a good thing. Relying on one man could leave you flat on your face, as she'd discovered to her cost.

Jamie had already had one man walk out of his short life. She wasn't going to allow it to happen a second time by encouraging him to spend time with a man as notorious for his unwillingness to commit to relationships as Dino.

They were doing fine, the two of them. They were a great team. She was the one in control of their future.

But she couldn't shift the heavy weight of guilt

and she'd hovered for an extra five minutes at the school gates, fighting the temptation to seek out Freddie and tell him to stop torturing her child. She'd stood and watched Jamie, a tiny figure, swamped by his warm jacket. *The only boy in his class who wasn't bringing a Dad to Dad's Day.*

She'd wanted to go into the school and yell at them for being insensitive, but Jamie had begged her not to. Now she was wishing she'd overruled him.

Should she have rung the school? Freddie's mother? She worried about it all the way to work and was still worrying when she visited Harry in the observation ward. He was in a corner bed on his own. 'Hey, layabout. I thought I'd say hi before I start work.'

His face brightened when he saw her. 'Wolf-girl!'

'Better not call me that. They're funny about animals in hospital—they might throw me out. Here…' Meg handed him a book she'd bought from the hospital shop, 'I've no idea if you've read it, but I thought it had an interesting cover. Monsters ripping people apart. Perfect teenage reading.'

'Thanks. Cool.' Harry put it on his lap and

reached for some chocolate from his locker. 'Want some?'

'At nine in the morning? No, thanks. I don't mind being wolf-girl, but I draw the line at elephant-girl, and if I start eating chocolate for breakfast that's what I'll be. How's your head?'

'Hurts.' Harry chewed. 'But they did that scan thing and said my brain is all right.'

'I know. No skull fracture. I rang last night to check up on you.' She looked at his bedside table. 'Who bought you the torch and the whistle? Your mum?'

'Are you kidding? Mum's never going to let me out of her sight again.' He looked gloomy. 'No, the torch and whistle were from Dr Zinetti. He dropped them off before he went off duty last night. Or it might have been this morning—it was definitely after midnight.'

He'd been at the hospital that late? Meg's tummy gave a little lurch. 'I suppose your mum was upset.'

'She freaked out. I'm grounded. No more walks on my own. Dad went totally mental.' He looked so forlorn that Meg took pity on him.

'When you've healed, you can walk with Rambo and me.'

'And me.' The deep, male voice came from right behind her and Meg felt her heart bump against her chest. Was it the Italian accent? Or the fact that last night he'd got too close for comfort? Or was it just her mother's fault for mentioning sex?

She closed her eyes briefly, feeling sick at the thought of telling him Jamie's request. Imagining how he would interpret such an invitation, Meg slid lower in her chair. Could anything be more embarrassing?

'Hi, Dr Zinetti,' Harry grinned. 'Thanks again for the torch and the whistle.'

'Basic walking equipment.' Dino sat down on the chair on the opposite side of Harry's bed and helped himself to chocolate. 'I'm going to run a survival course in the New Year. I've booked you on it, no charge.'

Harry sank back against the pillows. 'No way will Mum let me go to that.'

'Meg will speak to her.' Dino winked at her. 'Put in a good word. She's going to be taking a session on training a search dog.'

Meg recoiled. 'No, I'm not. No way am I standing up in front of a bunch of strangers and—'

'You're an important part of the MRT. We want

you there.' Railroading over her objections, he ate another piece of chocolate. 'And you're an expert at what you do.'

'Yes, well, just because you're good at something it doesn't mean you can talk about it. I'm useless at speaking in public.' She hated being looked at. Hated being the focus of attention. 'My tongue ties itself in a knot.'

'Does it, now?' his gaze slid to her mouth and lingered. 'I'm a doctor. I could look into that for you if you like.'

Was he flirting with her?

Meg felt her cheeks turn a fiery red. No, he wasn't. Men didn't flirt with her. They slapped her on the shoulders and offered to buy her a drink. She was one of the lads. Hating herself for feeling flustered, she scowled. 'I can't speak to large groups.'

'That's fine, because I'm thinking a maximum of ten. And then we're going to do some practical sessions outside. How to survive a night in the mountains, that sort of thing. We need you and Rambo for that. The work of the search-and-rescue dog is important.'

Meg wanted to tell him that anything other than one on one was a large group in her book, but she didn't want to look like a wimp. Although with strangers she definitely *was* a wimp. 'I'd be rubbish. I wouldn't have a clue what to say.'

'We'll work it out together.' Something in his frank, appraising gaze made it hard to breathe and Meg forgot about Harry, who was happily munching his way through a chocolate bar in the bed right next to them. She forgot that she'd been awake all night worrying about Jamie and Dad's Day. Because of the way Dino was looking at her, she forgot everything.

A warmth spread through her limbs and Meg was aware of every beat of her heart. And then he smiled.

At her.

Her insides melted.

The corners of her mouth flickered and she was about to smile back at him when a soft, feminine voice came from behind her.

'Dr Zinetti. It's so good to see you again—is there anything I can do for you?'

Meg turned to find the ward sister smiling at Dino. She knew her vaguely. Melissa someone or other. Always giggling with the crowd of girls from Radiography.

Staring at the woman's freshly glossed mouth

and smooth hair, the feeling of excitement left her. A cold feeling spread through her body. Turning away quickly, Meg dipped her head, feeling really awkward and furious with herself for being so stupid.

Dino hadn't been smiling at her.

He'd been smiling at Melissa, standing behind her. And it didn't take a genius to see why.

Melissa was the sort of woman who men found interesting. She was someone who took the trouble to straighten her hair before an early shift and apply lip gloss whenever a good-looking doctor walked onto the ward. Her uniform was slightly shorter than regulation, but not quite short enough to draw comment.

She was exactly like gorgeous Georgina.

Feeling the past rushing forwards to mock her, Meg suddenly wanted nothing more than to escape. The world was full of women like Melissa, she knew that all too well, just as she knew that the world was full of men who salivated over smooth hair, perfect nails and glossy lips.

Suddenly she felt grubby and unkempt. She was wearing the scrub suit she always wore for work in the emergency department—no doubt Dino was making several unflattering comparisons.

Her palms damp and her heart thudding, she shot to her feet and gave Harry a quick smile. 'I'm off. Be good.' She didn't look at Dino. He was probably occupied ogling Melissa's glossy mouth and, for some reason she didn't want to examine too closely, she didn't want to witness that.

'I heard about your heroic rescue, Dino,' Melissa was saying, and Meg quickened her pace as she walked towards the door. Within minutes they'd blatantly be arranging where and when to meet. Then Melissa would be giggling with her colleagues, planning what to wear.

Feeling as though she belonged to a different species, Meg hurried along the corridor towards the emergency department.

What had possessed her to promise Jamie she'd invite Dino to Dad's Day?

It was a totally ridiculous idea. And it wasn't going to happen.

No way. There were a million easier ways to make a complete fool of yourself.

She was going to have to find a different solution to Jamie's problem.

'Meg, wait—' Wondering what had caused her to run this time, Dino strode after her as she sped towards the door. He caught up with her easily and grabbed her arm. 'Wait! I want to talk to you.'

'I have to get to work.' Without looking at him, she shrugged him off and carried on walking. Her mouth was tight and she looked as if she was going into battle.

With a soft curse he caught up with her again and this time spun her round to face him, his hands hard on her shoulders.

Forced to stop, she made an impatient sound in her throat. 'What?' Her eyes were darkened by anger. It was like looking at the sea before a storm and Dino racked his brains to think what he could have done to whip up such a response from her. He'd always unsettled her, of course. He knew that, and he'd been biding his time. *Treading carefully.* Letting her get used to being around him.

For a moment he was tempted to tell her in blunt phrases exactly what it was he wanted from her, but his experience with women had taught him when to speak and when to go slow. With Meg Miller he was moving so slowly he was virtually standing still. *One step forwards, two steps back.* 'Why did you run off?'

'I didn't "run" anywhere. I have to get to work, so I left.'

In the middle of a conversation. In the middle of the first intimate exchange they'd ever shared. She'd been about to smile at him. For the first time since he'd met her eight months earlier, she'd almost acknowledged the connection between them. And then it had snapped. She'd snapped it.

It was like trying to tame a wild animal, he thought. You just had to be patient and let them come to you.

Shame that he wasn't that patient.

'Your Jamie is a great boy.' He stuck to a safe subject. 'He loves cars so much. I was the same at his age.' He'd expected her to relax, but instead the mention of her son seemed to increase her tension.

'Thanks for indulging his interest and letting him sit in your Lamborghini.' She was stiff and polite. 'That was kind of you when you must have had a million better things to do with your time.'

What was it about him that scared her? 'I wasn't being kind. I like his company. He's a great kid. You're a great mum. He's lucky.'

She stared at him for a moment and suddenly, out of nowhere, a sheen of tears veiled her eyes. Without saying anything, she jerked her shoulder away from his grasp and started walking again.

Cursing in Italian, Dino followed her. '*Accidenti*, will you stand still for one moment? *Mi dispiace*, if I upset you, I'm sorry, but I don't understand how. Jamie *is* a great kid and you *are* a great mum.' He blocked her path and she wrapped her arms around herself and stared past him, not meeting his eyes.

'Thanks.' She was all rigid formality. 'Is that what you wanted to say? Because I have to—'

'No.' He ignored the fact that they were standing in a busy corridor with half the hospital staff hurrying past. 'Why do you always run from me, Meg? I know you're not a coward. You were out there last night in howling winds, staring down at a vertiginous drop and you didn't even quiver.' He was still stunned by how well she'd handled the conditions on the mountain the previous night. But now there was no sign of the guts and bravery she'd shown in a blizzard. She looked jumpy and distracted, as if she had a thousand problems on her mind and no idea how to handle any of them. 'If we're talking about work or mountains, you have plenty to say, but when I change it to something more social, you clam up. Why?'

'Sorry. I'll try to be more sociable.' Her smile was false. 'It looks like we might have more snow. I do hope that won't make your drive to work difficult, Dr Zinetti.'

Curbing his exasperation, Dino stared down at her, studying the smooth skin of her cheek and the way her lips curved. 'I don't want to talk about the weather.'

'Sorry. We'll talk about something else. How did you like my mother's soup?'

'The soup was delicious. She obviously knows what hungry climbers need when they come home.'

She relaxed slightly. 'She ought to. Both my dad and my grandfather were in the mountain rescue team.'

He already knew that from the other guys, but he didn't say so. Instead he felt a buzz of triumph that reserved, buttoned-up Meg Miller had finally revealed something personal about herself. 'So it's in the family.' Dino moved to one side as the chief pharmacist hurried past. 'Same with me. My dad used to be a mountain guide. He took people up the Matterhorn.' *Give something back. Conversation. To and fro. Try and get her to relax.*

Her brow furrowed. 'The Matterhorn is in Switzerland.'

'Part of it is in Switzerland. The best part is in Italy. You're lucky you have your mum to help you. Jamie's lucky to have such close family.' He hesitated, wondering how far he dared push it. 'Does he ever see his father? Are you still in touch?'

He watched, cursing himself as her expression changed and her body tensed.

'No. All he has is me. So he's not that lucky, is he? And I really don't understand why everyone is taking this sudden interest in my love life.' Her voice rose and he saw the sudden flare of anguish in her eyes, which was rapidly replaced by horror that she'd revealed so much. Within seconds it was masked and she was businesslike. 'I really have to go.' Dodging him, she hurried along the corridor towards the emergency department, leaving Dino standing in silence, regretting bringing up the subject of Jamie's father.

He'd touched a nerve.

And he still hadn't asked her what he wanted to ask her. He'd had the tickets in his office for six months and he'd known instantly who he wanted to take. And he'd been waiting for the right moment to invite her.

A wry smile touched his mouth and the smile was at his own expense because this was the first time in his life he'd ever had to ask a woman a question and not been sure of the answer.

Determined to catch up with her and finish the conversation, he strode into the department and was immediately met by Ellie, one of the sisters in charge of the emergency unit.

'Oh, thank goodness!' She grabbed his arm and pushed a set of notes into his hand. 'Three-month-old baby with severe breathing difficulties—I've taken her into Paediatric Resus. Mum's demented with worry. Meg's already there because you know how good she is with babies and worried mothers.'

So there would be no chance to finish their conversation for the next hour or so, Dino thought grimly as he strode towards Resus. But later…

He pushed open the door and immediately picked up the tension in the atmosphere. Meg had already attached the baby to a cardiac monitor and a pulse oximeter and was giving oxygen. Despite the obvious crisis, her voice was gentle and soothing as she talked to the mother, explaining what she was doing. For a fraction of a second Dino watched her, transfixed by the change in her. There was no sign of the prickly, defensive exterior she showed to the world. With the baby and the mother, she was gentle and warm. Infinitely reassuring. If he'd been brought in to the department injured, he would have wanted Meg by his side. Once again he remembered how good she'd been with Harry. It was as if she lowered her guard around people who were vulnerable while the rest of the time she hid behind layers of thick armour plating.

'It happened to me,' she was saying. 'My Jamie was exactly three months old, just like Abby here. The oxygen levels in Abby's blood aren't quite as high as we'd like and she's really having problems with her breathing, poor thing, that's why I'm giving her some oxygen right now.'

'Did your son recover?' The mother's voice wavered and Meg reached across and gave her shoulder a squeeze.

'Celebrated his seventh birthday last week. Cheeky as ever. Addicted to superheroes. Batman, Superman, Spiderman—you name it. He saves the world at least a hundred times a day. Ah—here's Dr Zinetti right now.'

Dino strode into the room, noticing that Meg's anxiety and stiffness appeared to have vanished. She even looked pleased to see him.

Whatever else she might think of him, at work they were a good team.

'Dino, she's had a cold and runny nose for twenty-four hours and it's been getting steadily worse. She hasn't fed at all today, she has nasal discharge and a wheezy cough. Sats are ninety-four per cent so I've started her on oxygen because I can see she's struggling.'

'I can't believe how quickly she's got worse.' Abby's mother looked terrified, her face almost grey from lack of sleep and worry. 'Is she going to be all right?'

'I'm going to take a look at her right now.' Dino gently lifted the baby's vest so that he could look at her chest. He watched for a moment, noticed that the chest was visibly hyperinflated and that there were signs of intercostal recession. 'Was she born at full term?' He asked the mother a number of questions and then listened to the baby's chest.

'Is she bad?' The mother was hovering, stressed

out of her mind. 'I'm worrying that I should have brought her in sooner but I thought it was a cold.'

'You've done the right thing. Because she is little and she has tiny airways, she is struggling at the moment.' Dino folded the stethoscope. 'I can hear crackles in her lungs, which suggests that this could be bronchiolitis. It's a respiratory infection caused by a virus. It's quite common at this time of year. There's nothing you could have done to prevent it.'

She looked at him, desperate for reassurance. 'You're sure?'

'Positive. But in Abby's case it is quite severe so I'm going to run some tests and keep her on oxygen for now. I'm also going to contact the paediatric team because she's going to need to be admitted for a short time.'

'She needs to stay in hospital? It's nearly Christmas.'

'Hopefully it will only be for a few days.' Meg's voice was gentle. 'She's having to work quite hard to breathe, and if she isn't feeding then we need to keep her here and give her some help. Honestly, it's the best place for her to be. Whatever treatment she needs, we can give it right here. You know you wouldn't be able to relax if she was ill like this at home. You'd be hanging over her cot, listening to her every breath and just worrying.'

'Oh, yes, that's exactly what I've been doing.' The baby's mother looked dazed. 'I need to phone my husband—he's gone into work. He didn't realise she was this bad—neither of us did.'

'Why don't you do that right now? We're going to take some blood samples,' Dino took the tray that Meg had already prepared. 'That will help us work out exactly what's wrong with her and how we're going to treat her.'

'You're going to stick needles in her?' The mother looked appalled, her eyes full of tears. 'I should be there for her, hold her...'

Dino took one look at her ashen face and knew that if she stayed, she'd probably pass out. He was about to say something when Meg spoke.

'I think the most important thing right now is to call your husband. That's a bigger priority. You need the support. The weather isn't great out there so it might take him a while to get here. I'll hold Abby while Dr Zinetti takes the bloods.'

In one sentence she'd given the mother permission to leave and not to feel guilty. Admiring her skill, Dino waited while Abby's mother left the room. 'You're so good with worried mothers.'

'There's nothing worse than watching someone stick needles into your child. Can I ask why you're taking bloods? I got the tray ready just in case, but we don't usually do that for bronchiolitis. I thought it was a clinical diagnosis.'

'I want to check her blood gases. She has marked chest wall retraction, nasal flaring, expiratory grunting and her sats are dropping, despite the oxygen.'

'She's certainly a poorly girl.' Meg slid her hand over the baby's downy head. 'All right, sweetie, we're going to do this together and Uncle Dino is going to get that nasty needle in first time and not miss.'

'No pressure, then.' Dino ran his finger over the baby's tiny wrist and arm. 'If I manage it first time, I get to choose the time and the place.'

'For what?' She handed him a tourniquet.

'For our first date.'

Her cheeks flushed, Meg squeezed the baby's arm gently. 'I don't go on dates.'

Neither did he. Usually. He wondered what she'd say if she knew he was every bit as wary as she was. For the past two years he'd kept his relationships superficial. It was a measure of how much he liked Meg Miller that he was willing to risk the next step. 'Perhaps it's time you did.' Dino stroked his finger over the baby's skin, found what he wanted. Smoothly and confidently he slid the tiny needle into the vein. 'There. First time. I win the challenge.' He murmured softly to the baby in Italian and glanced up to find her watching him.

'I'm glad.' Her cheeks were flushed. 'I would have hated you to have missed, but I don't want you to take that the wrong way.' Meg turned her head to check the baby's pulse and blood pressure on the monitor. 'She really is very sick. I've rung PICU and warned them that they'll need to isolate her.'

Dino took the samples he needed and dropped them onto the tray, his eyes on the baby. 'I'm still not happy with her breathing. She may have to be ventilated.'

'Paediatric team on the way, including the anaesthetist.'

'The problem with working with you,' Dino drawled, 'is that you're so efficient there is no opportunity for me to impress you.'

'You got the needle in first time—that impressed

me. And anyway…' she pulled a sticker from a sheet in the notes and stuck it onto the form for the blood test, '…you don't need praise from me. You already have quite a fan club going, Dr Hot. I gather fourteen nurses have asked you to the Christmas ball so far. Is that all the bloods?'

This would have been the perfect moment to ask what he wanted to ask, but the situation was too tense to contemplate having a personal discussion. Later, he promised himself. Later, when they weren't working, he was going to remind her that she owed him a date. And no doubt she would fight him all the way.

In the eight months he'd worked at the hospital he'd noticed that Meg didn't really socialise. She worked and then she went home to her son. On the few occasions she joined the rest of the mountain rescue team for a drink, it was either early, in which case she took Jamie with her, or it was late and she popped in quickly while her mother was babysitting. At first he'd wondered if her attitude was driven by financial concerns, but as he'd got to know her better he'd realised that there was a great deal more to Meg's hermit-like existence than an urge for thrift.

Someone had hurt her. Presumably Jamie's father.

Relationships, he thought. *Complex and difficult.*

He watched as she moved around the room, calm, quiet and efficient. When it came to work, she never failed to impress him. What surprised him was the difference between her confidence levels in a work or rescue situation and her confidence levels in a social situation.

Abby's mother arrived back in the room at the same time as the paediatric team and Dino pushed aside thoughts of Meg, briefing his colleagues as they transferred the sick baby to PICU. He was walking back to Resus when Meg grabbed him and dragged him into an empty cubicle.

'About this date,' she whispered fiercely, her gaze flickering to the door to check no one was passing, 'there is somewhere I really want to go and I'd really like you to take me.'

Astonished that it had proved that easy, Dino smiled. '*Molto bene,*' he purred. 'Of course. Anything. Romantic dinner? Or something less public perhaps. I could cook for you. My place.'

Instead of reacting the way he expected, she chewed her lower lip nervously for a few seconds.

'I want you to come to my house at eight-thirty on Thursday morning.'

Dino watched her carefully. He could see the pulse beating in her throat. *Feel her nerves.* 'I'm all for injecting variety into the dating scene, *belissima*, but isn't eight-thirty in the morning a slightly unusual time to eat dinner? Unless you're suggesting breakfast?'

'Don't get any ideas. We won't be eating anything.' She pushed her hair out of her eyes and he noticed that her hand was shaking. 'Look, I know you won't want to do this, but—' She sucked in a deep breath, like someone summoning up courage to do something they found terrifying. '—Thursday is Dad's Day at school and Jamie doesn't have anyone to take. I know you're not his dad but that doesn't matter because it just has to be an important man in his life, and I know you're not exactly important, but—'

Dino covered her lips with his fingers. 'Meg, take a breath.'

'Sorry. Look, I'm sorry I asked—just forget it.'

'I'm glad you asked. And the answer is yes. Of course I'll go to Dad's Day with Jamie. I'd be honoured.'

'You would?' She stared up at him, her breathing rapid against his fingers. 'You'll go? Seriously?'

'Yes. Of course. I think he's a great kid.' It took a huge effort of will to remove his fingers from her soft lips. An even bigger effort not to replace them with his mouth. 'Just tell me what's expected of me.'

'I have absolutely no idea. All I know is that you have to be incredibly impressive,' she blurted out, 'so that Freddie stops telling him he's a loser because his dad doesn't want to see him.'

Dino felt anger flash. 'Some kid is calling him a loser?' *Was that the reason for the tears he'd seen in her eyes earlier?* 'Someone is bullying Jamie?'

'I don't think so. Not really. Hard to tell. The line between bullying and boy behaviour can be blurred.' She rubbed her fingers with her forehead, her eyes tired. 'I'm trying to stay calm and rational about it. But I've discovered that rational thinking goes out of the window when it's your child. Kids are really mean. And I know I have to get my head round it and in the end Jamie has to find his own way of dealing with it, but…' Her voice was thickened as she struggled not to break down. 'He's so little, and when it's your child it feels *horrible,* you have no idea. I just want to go and find Freddie and yell at him, but I can't do that.'

'Describe him to me,' Dino said coldly. 'I'll do it for you.'

'No.' With a tiny smile, she shook her head. 'What I want you to do is make Freddie and his dad look as small and insignificant as possible, while making yourself look like a cross between Mr Incredible and Batman.'

He raised an eyebrow. 'Does that mean I have to wear a tight red Lycra suit and a black cloak?'

She gave a choked laugh. 'You'd be arrested. I don't know what's the matter with me. I don't really want to make Freddie and his dad look small, and I *hate* myself for having to ask you to go so that Jamie can be like the other kids. I've always taught him that he doesn't have to be like everyone else—that people are allowed to be individuals—and here I am playing some silly game of impressing people.'

'Well, that's a great theory,' Dino drawled, 'but I guess sometimes it's just nice not to have to fight the world on everything.' And that was what she did. He was sure of it. She was standing between the world and her child. 'I'll do it, Meg. No problem. I can't promise red Lycra, but I do promise to help Jamie. Will you be there?'

'No. Mums aren't allowed. I'll be outside, biting my nails.'

He took her hand in his and lifted it—and had a brief glimpse of bitten nails before she snatched her hand away, her cheeks pink.

'I thought you could pick him up from home...' She thrust her hands behind her back. '...in your Batmobile. That should attract some serious attention at the school gates.'

'Particularly if it carries on snowing. The Lamborghini is a nightmare in the snow. I'm likely to crash right through the school gates if the conditions don't improve and that isn't exactly superhero behaviour, but I'll see what I can do. You really do want to give them the full treatment, don't you? In return,' Dino drawled, 'you'll do something for me.'

The relief in her eyes was replaced by caution. 'What?'

'This isn't our date. Next time it's my choice. We go where I decide, when I decide. And it won't be at eight-thirty in the morning, Meg, so you'll need to book a babysitter.'

He'd been patient long enough.

CHAPTER THREE

'Mum, he was *awesome*. When he stripped off his jacket he was wearing this tight suit *just* like Mr Incredible, and he was all muscle, and Freddie's mouth was like this...' Jamie dropped his jaw to show her. 'And he had a proper six-pack and everything and then he was telling us about the suit and he said that you need to wear that for speed so that you go as fast as possible when you're skiing. He wore it in the Olympics! You should have seen Freddie's face when Dino got out his gold medal. He opened and closed his mouth like a fish and his dad sort of spluttered a bit and went very red in the face and quiet.' Jamie chatted non-stop while he sprinkled glitter onto the Christmas card he was making. 'And then he talked about when he worked as a mountain guide in Italy, where he comes from, and there was this avalanche...'

Listening to Jamie talk, Meg felt a rush of gratitude towards Dino. Whatever he'd said and done at Dad's Day, it had obviously been the right thing.

'Don't use too much glue or the card will be sticky.'

He stared at the card dubiously. 'Do you think Grandma is going to like this? We could have bought one.'

'Home-made is better. She's going to love it. So what else happened?'

'All the kids thought his Lamborghini looked *exactly* like the Batmobile.' Jamie added stars to the card. 'And he let me wear his Olympic medal.'

He'd let him wear his Olympic medal? *Wasn't that going a bit over the top?*

'So, anyway, I invited him over for pizza night, Mum.'

'Who?'

'Dino, of course.'

'You invited him for pizza night?'

'Yes. Pizza is Italian, isn't it? He told me he likes pizza.'

Trying to reconcile the smooth, sophisticated Dino she knew with a version that ate pizza, especially *her* pizza, Meg closed her eyes.

Feeling as though she was being sucked into

quicksand, she picked up the tube of glitter. 'He wouldn't want to come over, sweetheart. He was probably just being polite.'

Jamie's smile faded. 'You mean he doesn't really like us?'

'No, he likes us,' Meg said quickly, 'of course he likes us. Especially you. I *know* he likes you a lot. I'm just saying that a man like Dino is busy, and he's probably got better things to do than eat pizza with us.'

'So why did he say he's really looking forward to it? And it isn't just me he likes—he likes you a lot too, Mum. He kept asking stuff about you all the time while we were in the car. Do you think he wants to marry you and have sex? Is it because Grandma and I hung extra mistletoe from the door?'

The glitter slipped through her fingers. 'No— no, I don't think that's what he's thinking and I don't think the mistletoe makes any difference. What do you mean, he was asking stuff about me? What kind of stuff?'

'Mostly questions about what you do when you're not working. I told him I'm a lot of work, so when you're not working or out on a rescue, you're usually looking after me. Mum, there's glitter all over the floor.'

Meg started to clean it up. 'Well, it's certainly true that I'm usually looking after you. Apart from the fact you eat enough for eight boys, you create masses of laundry. I couldn't believe the state of your rugby kit this week.' She kept talking so that she didn't over-analyse the fact that Dino had been asking about her. 'Did you leave any mud on the field?'

'Freddie tackled me. He pushed me right into the mud.'

Freddie again. 'Well, maybe Freddie won't be so quick to jump on you now he knows your best friend is a superhero.' She emptied glitter into the bin. 'So what night did you invite Dino? Just so that I make sure there is some pizza for him to eat.'

'Tomorrow, because it's a Friday and pizza night is always Friday. And he's expecting your extra-gooey chocolate cake. I told him it's the only other thing you can cook.'

'Right.' This was a man who dined out in the finest restaurants. His favourite food was probably lobster. And she was giving him pizza and chocolate cake. In a house festooned with mistletoe.

* * *

'Thanks so much for what you did yesterday.' In the middle of the constant bustle of the emergency department, Meg handed Dino a set of notes to sign. 'You made Jamie's week. Actually, you probably made his year. The whole class is talking about your car and your Mr Incredible suit. I must admit I find it surprising you can still fit in a suit you wore when you were nineteen.'

'It was a tight fit.' Dino scrawled his signature on the page. 'I've filled out since then.'

She looked at his shoulders and then looked away again quickly. 'I can imagine.'

'Send this guy to fracture clinic. Did that man in cubicle 4 get transferred?'

'They found him a bed on the medical ward.' She wasn't going to think about his shoulders. 'Dino, it was really sweet of you to tell Jamie that you love pizza, but you really don't have to torture yourself like that. I'm honestly not expecting you to come. I'll make some excuse—tell him you had some emergency or something.'

'No, you won't.' Frowning, Dino rose to his feet and slid his pen into his pocket. 'I love pizza. I'm looking forward to it. And I think Jamie is great. He has a good sense of humour and he's very observant about people. And I'm looking forward to your food.'

'All right, that is *seriously* bad news.' Meg gulped. 'I ought to warn you that I am not that great a cook. Pizza is about the limit of my repertoire, and I only manage that because Jamie's pretty good with toppings. He gives me a list and I buy them and then he just throws them on. He even tells me when it's cooked. If he left it to me, the whole thing would be burned.'

'Are you trying to put me off?'

'I'm just warning you that this isn't going to be a gourmet evening. I'm sure you're wishing you'd never said yes.' Of course that was what he was wishing. He must be desperate to back out. Why would a good-looking, single guy want to waste a precious evening off eating home-made pizza with a seven-year-old boy and his mother? 'I know how persuasive Jamie can be and it was kind of you not to hurt his feelings but, seriously, it's OK. I'll handle it with him.'

'What time does pizza night start?'

Meg stared at him. 'Y-you're coming? Seriously?'

'I wouldn't miss it. What time?'

'Oh—er—indecently early. Six o'clock. Jamie goes to bed around eight so we have to eat around then. That's way too early for you, I'm sure, so maybe we should just—'

'Six it is.'

She looked at him helplessly. What was this all about? Why did he want to eat pizza at her house? *Why had he helped her child?* 'Dino—'

'Would you mind talking to the relatives of the child who fell off his bike? They're worried about their son being discharged home. They need a head injury information sheet and some of your special brand of "I'm-a-mother-too" reassurance.'

'Right. I'll do that.' He was behaving as if there was nothing strange about the fact that he was coming round for dinner. As if it were something they did all the time. She had no idea what was going through his mind. Unless it was the fact that her mother had yelled the word 'sex' across the whole valley and he thought he may as well make the most of what was on offer. Perhaps he'd decided that the mistletoe was some sort of hint. On the other hand, a man like Dino wasn't exactly going to find himself short of offers or opportunity. Mistletoe or no mistletoe, he didn't need to settle for a girl who didn't paint her nails.

One thing she knew for sure—once he'd tasted her food, he wouldn't be coming back for more.

Dino pulled up outside the cottage and tried to remember when he'd last eaten a meal at six o'clock in the evening. Locking the car, he smiled. *Probably the same time he'd last eaten pizza.*

Another fresh fall of snow had dusted the path and he saw a small pair of blue Wellington boots covered in pictures of Spiderman abandoned on the step.

As he waited for Meg to answer the door, he studied the wreath. It was a festive twist of ivy, pine cones and fat, crimson holly berries. Looking closer, he saw that it was just a bit haphazard, and suddenly had a vision of Meg and Jamie making it together, laughing at the kitchen table. A family preparing for Christmas.

He was eying the mistletoe thoughtfully when the door was dragged open and he was hit by light and warmth.

Jamie stood there, a grin on his face, Rambo wagging his tail by his side. 'You made it. Come in.' Unselfconscious, he grabbed Dino's hand and pulled him inside. 'You have to choose your topping. Pepperoni, olive, ham or mushroom. Usually

I'm only allowed to pick three but Mum might let you have more as you're the guest.'

Dino followed him into the kitchen and found Meg, red in the face, making pizzas on a scrubbed wooden table.

'Hi—you made it. That's great.' She looked flustered. White patches of flour dusted the front of her apron and the arms of her jumper. Her hair was clipped to the top of her head and tumbled around her face in a riot of haphazard curls.

Her eyes changed colour, he noticed, according to her mood. Tonight they were a deep, sparkling blue like one of the lakes on a summer's day. 'I bought you something to drink.' He held out the bottle and she looked at it and gave a hesitant laugh.

'Champagne? I don't know what you're expecting, Dino, but what we have here is a basic pizza with a few toppings. Nothing fancy.'

'Champagne goes with everything.' He looked around him. Her kitchen was warm and homely, delightfully haphazard, like everything else in her life. At one end of the table there was a stack of papers and unopened post, which she'd obviously cleared to one side in order to make the pizza. Brightly coloured alphabet magnets decorated the door of the fridge and the walls were adorned with Jamie's paintings and photographs.

Intrigued, Dino strolled across the room to take a closer look. There were photographs of Meg and Jamie wrestling in the snow. One of Jamie in his school uniform, looking proud. Jamie and Rambo. Meg and Rambo. A family.

Something pulled inside him and suddenly he felt cold, despite the warmth thumping from the green range cooker that was the heart of the kitchen. This was what a childhood was supposed to be like. A million small experiences, explored together and retained for ever in the memory. A foundation for life. In comparison to the rich tapestry of family life spread around the kitchen, his own experience seemed barren and empty. His mother had paid expensive photographers to record various carefully selected moments and the subsequent pictures had been neatly catalogued and stored. Whatever artwork he'd brought home from school had been swiftly disposed of because his mother had hated clutter of any sort. The walls of his home had also been adorned with priceless paintings that no one could touch. His mother would no more have displayed one of his childish drawings than she would be seen without her make-up.

Pushing aside that bitter thought, Dino opened a glass-fronted cupboard and helped himself to two tall stemmed glasses.

As he popped the cork on the champagne, he realised that Meg was watching him as she shaped dough into rounds.

'Sorry, we're in a bit of a mess.'

'I like it.' He poured champagne into the glasses. 'This is a lovely cottage. How long have you lived here?'

'The house belonged to my grandfather. When he died my dad fixed it up and then they rented it to tourists for a while. Then I had Jamie and needed somewhere to live, so they stopped renting it out and it became mine. I love it here. The views are incredible, the walking is fantastic and in the summer we sail on the lake, don't we, Jamie?'

'Grandma bought me my own boat. It's a single-hander.' Jamie climbed onto a stool. 'Do you like boats, Dino?'

'I've never had much to do with boats.' He put a glass of champagne down next to her hand. 'But I know I'd love sailing.'

'Sometimes I capsize. That's the best part.'

Meg finished the last pizza base and gave a sigh of relief, as if preparing the food had been a test she'd faced and passed. 'OK, guys, over to you.' She pushed two of the bases across the table towards them and picked up her glass. 'Cheers. What do you say in Italy?'

'*Salute!*'

Her glass made a gentle ringing sound as she tapped it against his. '*Salute.* To superheroes and pizza night.' She sipped the champagne. 'Oh, that's so good. I've never tasted anything like it. Where did you get it from? Is it expensive?'

'I picked it up last time I was home,' Dino avoided the question, putting the open bottle in the fridge. He looked at his pizza base. 'I'm going to need some help here, Jamie. Do you have any advice for me?'

Jamie was holding a bowl of tomato sauce. 'I can do yours for you if you like.'

'That would be great, thanks. You obviously have more experience than me.' Dino sat down on a chair, watching Meg. Her face was pink from shaping dough and a few more wisps of blonde hair had escaped from the clip on her head. He'd seen her handle the most complex medical situations without working up a sweat, but here in the kitchen, she was definitely sweating.

'OK, Jamie, I'm ready for tomato.' She pushed her pizza base towards her son. 'You know what to do. Not too much or you'll make it soggy.'

Dino leaned across and helped himself to an olive. 'So how was school today, Jamie? Any trouble from Freddie?'

'Nope. Not today.' Jamie carefully spread tomato sauce on the three pizzas. 'He wants to be my friend now.'

'That's good.'

'Not really. It's only because he wants a ride in your car.' Jamie picked up a bowl of grated cheese and Dino looked at Meg. She was staring at her son and there was so much love in her eyes that he felt something squeeze his insides.

'You're pretty wise about people for someone who is only seven years old. I wish I'd known that much at your age.'

Jamie pulled a face. 'Yesterday he didn't want to be my friend, and today he does. I haven't changed. The only thing that's changed is that he knows you're my friend.'

'That doesn't matter, Jamie.' Meg's voice was

husky. 'As long as he isn't being nasty, that's the important thing.'

'I think the reason he picks on me is so that he doesn't get picked on himself.'

Startled by that insight, Dino put down his glass. 'What makes you say that?'

'The way people behave…' Jamie sprinkled cheese over the pizza bases. 'There's usually a reason. My mum taught me that. People are complicated. What you see on the outside isn't what's on the inside.'

'Right.' Dino looked at Meg but she was busy chopping mushrooms.

'You can't always believe what people say,' Jamie said stoutly, plopping olives and pepperoni onto one of the pizzas. 'Sometimes people say things they don't mean. And sometimes they don't say things they do mean. Do you want pepperoni and olives?'

'*Sì, grazie,*' Dino said absently, his mind on the conversation. *Sometimes people say things they don't mean.* Was that what had happened with Jamie's father? 'So who is your best friend at school?'

'Luke Nicholson.'

'Sean and Ally's youngest son.' Meg took

another sip of her champagne. 'Luke is a really nice boy. Sean's been taking the two of them climbing. Jamie, that's enough for one pizza. Do one of the others now.'

Jamie loaded the other pizza bases with toppings. 'If we lived in Italy, could we eat this all the time? I bet you made loads of pizzas with your parents when you were little, Dino.'

Dino thought about the atmosphere of his parents' home. On the rare occasions he'd been allowed to join his parents for dinner, it had been an excruciatingly formal occasion with no concession to the presence of children. His sister and he had endured countless long, boring evenings when he would rather have been playing or asleep.

'I didn't make pizza, but I always wanted to.' At the time he hadn't imagined that kids did that sort of thing with their parents, but clearly he was wrong.

Jamie pushed a base across to him. 'Go on, then. The cheese and tomato is the hard part and I've done that for you. You just have to choose what else you want.'

Smiling, Dino sprinkled olives, pepperoni and mushrooms and Meg slid the pizzas into the oven.

Jamie jumped down from his stool. 'I'm going to watch TV until it's ready. Don't let them burn, Mum.' He vanished from the room and Meg gave Dino an apologetic glance.

'Sorry.' She started clearing the various bowls from the table. 'Not what you're used to, I'm sure.'

'No. It's better.'

'Don't patronise us, Dino.'

'Is that what you think I'm doing?'

'You just admitted you didn't eat pizza when you were a child.'

'Not because I didn't want to. Usually my sister and I ate alone in the kitchen with one of the nannies while my parents entertained in the dining room.' He looked around her kitchen. 'And the kitchen was nothing like this one.'

'You mean messy.'

'I mean homely.' He picked up one of Jamie's paintings that had been tidied to one side of the table. 'He's such an important part of your life. The evidence is everywhere.'

'That's because I don't spend enough time cleaning the place.' She blew the strands of hair away from her eyes. 'I'm not a natural housekeeper.'

'You're proud of him. It shows. And the place

looks fine to me. No kid wants to live in a mausoleum.'

Startled by the sudden abruptness in Dino's voice, Meg risked asking a personal question. 'Is that how your house felt when you were growing up?'

Dino pushed his chair away from the table and stretched out his legs. 'We had paintings wired to alarm systems that connected straight through to the police station. Once I brought half the Rome police force round to the house by kicking a football indoors.'

'Ah.'

'My parents' child-care strategy was that children shouldn't be seen or heard. Which meant that basically we lived separate lives.'

A tiny frown creased her brow. 'I admit that doesn't sound great.'

'It wasn't.' Dino spoke quietly, not wanting to disturb too many of the memories. 'So perhaps now you'll believe me when I say I'm enjoying pizza night.'

'Oh, well—good.'

'You do this every Friday?'

'Yes. Unless I'm working.' She washed her hands and removed her apron. 'I wanted to thank

you again for what you did yesterday. It's made all
the difference to Jamie. And to me. It was such
a relief to see him bouncing out of school today
instead of slinking along. I can always tell what
sort of day he's had by the way he walks out of
the building.'

'It was tough not intervening. I wanted to pick
Freddie up by the collar and give him a talking
to.'

'I think you found a more effective way of si-
lencing him. Hopefully it will all calm down
now.' Reaching up, she closed the blind in the
kitchen. 'It's snowing again. Did you hear that
they've issued an avalanche warning? Can you
believe that in the Lake District?'

'We have had half a metre of snow in some
places. Add to that a high wind and you end
up with drifts that are only loosely attached to
the mountainside. The snow pack needs time to
consolidate.'

'I suppose you're used to it, having been brought
up in the Alps. Apparently it's lethal underfoot.
Some of the edges are literally breaking away
and if you're standing underneath at the time,
you're in trouble. They're warning people not to
venture out. But people will, of course. There's

always someone who thinks they're cleverer than the weather.' The conversation was light, skating over the surface of the personal, but he felt the undercurrent of tension and he knew she felt it, too.

Since that moment in the tent on the mountain, everything had changed.

Every interaction they shared had another level—something deeper.

Sensing that this wasn't the moment to explore that further, Dino looked at the dog stretched out in front of the range cooker, enjoying the warmth. 'Is Rambo trained to search in snow?'

'Yes. Whenever we have snow we do extra training because obviously there aren't that many opportunities around here. But it's a different skill. A search dog is trained to find the person, bark, and then return to the handler. They carry on doing that until they've drawn the handler to the body.' She bent down and stroked Rambo's head, making a fuss of him. 'When they're working in snow they have to stay with the scent and dig. He's good at it.'

'How long have you had him?' Dino crouched down to stroke the dog too and Meg immediately pulled her hand away.

'He was my eighteenth birthday present from my parents. I was already involved with the mountain rescue team. I used to help out manning the base and I worked as a volunteer body. That means losing yourself on a mountain so that the dogs can practise finding you. Then, when I had Rambo, I trained him. It took longer than usual because halfway through I discovered I was pregnant and that—well, let's just say that complicated things.'

He wanted to ask her how, but he was afraid of triggering the same response he'd seen a few days earlier when he'd asked if Jamie's father was still on the scene. 'So you moved into this cottage?'

'My dad died the same year I had Jamie.' She pulled a face. 'It was a truly terrible year. I lived with Mum for a while, it worked better that way. We were both on our own and somehow we got through it together. Then she suggested I move into Lake Cottage. I'd always loved it and it's only half a mile from her house so it's perfect. If I'm called out in the night on a rescue I just drop Jamie with her, or she comes over here. I'm lucky. How about you? How did you get involved with mountain rescue?'

'When I stopped competitive skiing, I started

off working as a ski guide to earn money before I went to university. Then I did mountain rescue.'

He wanted to ask whether she'd been on her own right from the start. Whether Jamie's father had walked out before he was born. Had she married the guy?

'How did you end up in England?'

He'd been escaping. 'I wanted a change. Do I smell pizza?'

Meg gasped and grabbed a cloth. 'Jamie will kill me if I've burnt them.' She pulled them out of the oven and Dino smiled as he looked at the bubbling cheese and perfectly cooked crust.

'I thought you told me you were a lousy cook.'

'I am normally. You were the one who reminded me to get them out of the oven before they were burnt to a cinder.' She cut the pizzas into slices. 'Jamie! It's ready!'

They ate pizza together and he watched as she listened attentively to Jamie's questions and answered them. She was interested in her child, he thought, and that gave the boy confidence. He tried to remember a time when his mother had given him that much of her time, but failed.

Families were all different, but this—this was the way he would have wanted his to be.

After the pizza had been cleared away and Jamie had gone to get ready for bed, Dino decided that this was the right time to ask the question he'd been waiting to ask. 'I have two tickets to the Christmas ball.'

Her shoulders tensed. 'Good for you. I hope you have a nice time.'

'I'll pick you up at eight o'clock.'

It took a moment for his words to sink in, but when they did her entire face changed. The tension that had been simmering below the surface bubbled up. 'Me? No way. I don't go to that sort of thing.'

'Why not?'

'For a start, I don't dance.'

'Pathetic excuse.'

'That was just one. I have loads more. I can give you a list.'

'And I'm not going to be impressed by any of them.' Dino wondered why it was such a big deal to her. Judging from the expression on her face, he might have just asked her to have his babies.

Was it him? he wondered. *Or men in general?*

'The ball is next Saturday,' he said calmly, 'at the Winter Hill Hotel and Spa.'

'I know when it is and I've already told you I can't make it.' She stacked the dirty plates and took them over to the dishwasher. 'But thanks for inviting me. That was kind.'

'Kind?' Dino put his glass down slowly. 'Is that what you think? That I'm being kind?'

'I'm not thinking at all.' There was a note of panic in her voice as she clattered plates. 'There's no need to think and analyse because I'm not going. Take someone else. I'm sure there's a whole queue of women just desperate to go with you.' One of the plates slipped through her fingers and smashed on the floor. Muttering under her breath, she swept up the bits and disposed of them.

Dino stood up to help her but she glared at him. 'I'm fine—I can sweep up my own mess, Dino.'

'Do you always insist on doing everything by yourself, with no help?'

'Yes. I'm a grown-up. That's what happens when you're a grown-up. It's called independence.'

'Doesn't mean you can't take help.'

'I'm fine, Dino.'

He stood still, wondering what it was about him

that had her so on edge. She wasn't just uncomfortable around him—she was nervous. Jumpy. 'If I'd asked you out to dinner, would you have said yes?'

'Maybe… No…' She shook her head. 'No, I wouldn't. I don't date. It just isn't…'

'Isn't what?'

'Me. My life. Pick another woman, Dino.'

'I just picked you.'

'Well, unpick me!' Her eyes were two huge pools of panic. 'You'd have more fun with someone else. I'm not great at parties. I don't dance, I hate small talk and…' She flicked the wisps of hair out of her eyes with shaking fingers. 'Dino, just forget it. I don't even know why you're asking me.'

'Because you're the one I want to take. We don't have to dance if you don't want to. But that doesn't stop us going out. It's Christmas, Meg. Let your hair down.' He meant it in both a figurative and literal sense. He'd only seen her with her hair down once and that had been when she'd pulled her hat off her head the night they'd rescued Harry. The image of pale gold curls was still embedded in his brain. Using his powers of persuasion, he tried to think what might tempt her to go. 'It's a really smart evening. A good excuse to buy yourself a new dress.'

Another plate almost slipped to the floor but this time she caught it just in time. 'I don't need a new dress because I'm not going.'

Dino cursed himself for being tactless. She was a single mother, wasn't she? She probably had to watch her finances really carefully and here was he suggesting she buy a new dress. He wanted to offer to treat her to something new but sensed that would offend her well-developed sense of independence. Instead, he tried to rescue the situation. 'Just wear anything that's in your wardrobe.'

'Oh, right. I'll wear my best weatherproof jacket, shall I?' Her tone was light but her shoulders were rigid as she clattered around the kitchen, tidying surfaces that were already tidy. 'As I said, it's kind of you Dino, but, really, I don't want to go. You'll have loads more fun with someone else. I won't offer you coffee because I expect you're in a hurry to leave.'

And that was that.

The friendly atmosphere had shattered. The conversation had made her so uncomfortable that she wanted it to be over. She wanted him to leave.

Dino didn't budge. 'Coffee would be great. And I'm not in a hurry. So is it the issue of what to wear that's putting you off going? Because if so, I—'

'You don't give up, do you?' Her interruption was sharp. 'I've told you—that sort of thing just isn't me.'

'So what is you?'

She spooned fresh coffee into a jug. 'I play with my son and my dog. I work. I train Rambo. I walk in the mountains. That's it. That's my life. Maybe other people wouldn't find it exciting, but I love it. I don't need to dress up to enjoy myself. I'm happier in my walking boots than stilettos. Going to parties isn't on the list of things I do.'

Dino stood up and walked across to her, removed the spoon from her hand and put his hands on her shoulders. Rambo lifted his head, tongue lolling. Then his tail brushed over the floor, as if he approved.

'Why does it have to be one thing or another? You make it sound as though they're two different lives, but they could fit alongside each other. We had a deal, remember?' He cupped her face in his hands, stroking his thumb over her cheek, trying to read what was going on in her head. 'You owe me a date. Time of my choosing. Place of my choosing. Time is going to be next Saturday. Place is going to be the Christmas ball. And you're going to have a nice time. I promise you.'

'Don't you listen to "no"?'

'I'm selective.'

Her eyes gleamed with exasperation. 'Why are you asking me, anyway? Is Melissa busy?'

'Melissa?' Dino frowned. 'You mean the blonde who works in the observation unit? I have no idea if she's busy. I haven't asked her.'

'You should. Judging from the way she was flirting with you earlier in the week, I'm sure she'd say yes.'

'That's why you walked off so abruptly?'

'I didn't want to get in the way of a beautiful romance.' She pushed at his chest and he thought it was interesting that this time Rambo didn't growl a warning. Which was just as well because, dog or no dog, this time he wasn't moving.

'I'm not in a relationship with Melissa.'

'I couldn't care less if you are. It isn't any of my business.' The heat rushed into her cheeks and Dino found himself struggling to concentrate.

The scent of her hair numbed his reactions and the soft curve of her mouth pulled him in.

'You think I'd be asking you to the ball if I was seeing someone?'

'You're a popular guy. It's like a hornets' nest around your office on some days. The women are three deep.'

'I'm not involved with anyone.'

'So who did you take to dinner last Sunday?'

'Her name is Anna Townsend. She's a lawyer who has done some work for me in the past. And it was just lunch.'

'You said the date ended exactly the way you wanted it to.'

'It wasn't a "date" in the sense that you mean,' he said calmly, 'and it did end exactly the way I wanted it to. She went home and I went for a walk in the mountains.' Outside the snow might be falling but here, inside her kitchen, the heat was building between them.

Her breathing wasn't quite steady. 'It doesn't make any difference. I still can't go with you. Even if I wanted to, I wouldn't be able to arrange babysitting at this short notice.'

'Your mum is babysitting. I already asked her.'

Meg's mouth dropped open. 'You *asked* her? You've already asked my mum? Is this a conspiracy to get me into a dress or something?'

'Actually my long-term plan was to get you *out* of your dress.' Dino slid one hand into her hair, amused to see her so flustered. Her soft curls wrapped themselves around his fingers. 'Judging from your expression I gather flirting isn't on the list of things you usually do either. How about kissing, Meg?' He lowered his head so that his mouth almost touched hers. 'Is kissing on the list of things you do?' The tension hovered there between them, sharpened by the knowledge of what was to come. For a moment neither of them moved. Sexual chemistry arced through the stillness and he saw her lips part and her breathing grow shallow.

Losing his grip on control, Dino claimed her mouth in what was supposed to be a teasing, exploratory kiss, but the moment their lips touched it was like lighting a fuse. Heat ripped through his body and pulsed across nerve endings. It was scorching and wild and he heard her gasp. Her fingers clutched his shoulders and then she was kissing him back, her body yielding against his as he pressed her back against the cupboard.

'Mum!' Through the haze of passion, Jamie's voice came from upstairs. 'I'm ready for you to tuck me in!'

She jerked in his arms and Dino released her instantly. 'Sorry.' His voice came out rough and raw. 'Bad timing.'

'Yes…' She rubbed her fingers over her scarlet cheeks. 'You— How did you learn to—? Never mind.' Deliciously flustered, she moved away from him. 'I have to go and read to Jamie.'

'Go.' Dino thought about asking whether he could use her bathroom for a cold shower. 'I'll pour the coffee.'

'No. Perhaps we'd better call it a night.' She ran her tongue over her lower lip, her expression dazed. 'By the time I've read to him and tucked him in, you'll be bored. There's no point in you waiting around…' She looked confused, as if she wasn't quite aware of her surroundings, and he understood that feeling. He'd thought about kissing her for a long time, of course; since the first day he'd started working in the emergency department and had seen her talking some drunk out of hitting her. He'd had plenty of fantasies about tasting her smart mouth, but all those fantasies had just been blown apart and replaced by hot, pulsing reality. If Jamie hadn't called out when he had…

'All right, I'll go. This time.' His voice sounded husky. 'But next time, Meg, I won't be leaving before coffee.' Having delivered that warning, Dino grabbed his jacket from the back of the chair. 'Thanks for the pizza. I'll pick you up at eight o'clock on Saturday. And I'm not taking no for an answer.'

Meg banged into the doorframe and tripped over Jamie's schoolbag.

'Look where you're going, Mummy.' Jamie's voice was sleepy. 'You took a long time. Were you talking to Dino?'

Focus, Meg, focus. One foot in front of the other.

'Yes, we were talking. Just—talking.' Her mind still on Dino, Meg stooped to pick his schoolbag up off the floor, wondering how a single kiss could have a negative effect on balance. The world was hazy and there was a strange buzzing in her head. Maybe it was the champagne.

She ran her tongue over her lower lip again, still tasting the warmth of his kiss. Erotic images exploded in her brain.

'Mummy, why is your face all red?'

Because she was thinking of Dino. 'Because I've been rushing around making supper, pulling pizza out of the oven and generally slaving away all evening.' Turning her back to Jamie, she laid his clothes over the back of the chair, taking her time so that her face calmed down, telling herself that the only reason she felt this way was because she hadn't been kissed by a man for such a long time.

But was that really true?

Since when had she had a burning urge to rip a man's clothes off? When had she ever been so aware of a man, physically?

Cross with herself, she reminded herself about all the women who were interested in Dino. There were so many, she'd lost count. She wouldn't be human if she didn't notice how good looking he was. And as for kissing—well, no doubt Dino Zinetti had a PhD in kissing. Dr Hot indeed.

'Jamie, it's time for you to get some sleep.'

'Can't I have a story? You haven't read to me.'

Meg grabbed the book from the bed and sat down next to him. But instead of seeing the words, she saw the sexy look in Dino's eyes as he'd bent his head to kiss her.

It wasn't the champagne. It was the man.

Jamie sighed, wriggled upright and turned the book the other way up. 'You can't read if it's upside down, silly.'

Meg blinked. 'Oh. Just testing to see if you were concentrating.' She gave a weak smile and tried to focus on the page but her lips were tingling and her pulse was still racing. 'Right—where were we? Dragons…' She read the words aloud without digesting the meaning. *What now?* What was she supposed to say when she saw him at work? Was she going to behave as if nothing had happened? Would he? And what about the Christmas ball? She'd said no at least ten times, but Dino didn't listen to 'no'.

'You're not using the right voices. Normally you do a high voice for the baby dragon and a low voice for the big dragon.' Jamie peered at her. 'Are you sure you're OK? You look sort of weird. Did you bang your head when you walked into my door?'

She felt sort of weird.

She felt…different.

It was just a kiss, for goodness' sake. She rolled her eyes. That was like describing champagne as 'just a drink'. Who was she kidding? As kisses went, this one had blown every circuit in her mind. Judging from the way he hadn't argued about leaving, she guessed it had blown every circuit in his, too.

'I'm fine,' Meg said firmly, concentrating hard on the dragon story and trying desperately not to think about Dino. He shouldn't have complicated everything by kissing her, but they could move on from this. She wouldn't be going to the ball with him. The mere thought of it filled her with dread. It would show off all the worst parts of herself.

She knew that most of the girls working at the hospital looked forward to it all year. It was the highlight of the Christmas social calendar and there was always a fight for tickets and an argument over who was going to work and who was going to have the night off.

Meg didn't feel that way, which was why she always ended up working.

She gave a slow smile as the answer flew into her head. Of course. Why hadn't she thought of it before? She'd volunteer to work, as she always did every other year. If Dino wouldn't take no for an answer, she'd simply make herself unavailable.

CHAPTER FOUR

MEG was dressing the leg of an old lady who had slipped on the snow and ice when her team pager went off. 'Oh.' She looked down at herself. 'I'm bleeping, Agnes. That's the mountain rescue pager.'

'Someone in trouble on the mountains, dear? The snow was falling all night but I still see walkers trudging past my front door.' The woman flexed her foot. 'That feels very comfortable, thank you. You'd better see what they want, Meg. Don't mind me. I can get my own shoe back on.'

'Don't move until I've talked to you about how you're getting home, Agnes.' Meg dragged the pager out of her pocket and read the message. 'Avalanche? You have to be kidding me.'

'Worst weather conditions for eighteen years. I had to wait three hours for a bus yesterday.' Ignoring Meg's instructions, Agnes stood up. 'It isn't safe to leave the house without crampons.

And a young thing like you shouldn't be going out in all weathers. I remember your dad was the same.'

Meg washed her hands quickly. 'Agnes, if you come with me now, I can drop you off on my way to the mountain rescue base. I drive past your house. Then you won't have to stand in the freezing cold waiting for a bus that might never turn up because of the snow. I just need to tell the sister in charge what's happening. Wait there for me.'

She found Ellie, grabbed her coat and her car keys and minutes later she was dropping Agnes off outside her cottage. Having seen her safely inside the house, Meg drove to her mother's house, collected Rambo and made her way through the falling snow to the rescue centre.

'A party of three men were ski touring.' Sean, the leader of the local mountain rescue team, was standing over a map, pointing out the search area. 'They were traversing along the top of this gully when one of them was caught in an avalanche. Their last known position was here, but since then the battery on their cellphone has died, or else they've been caught by another avalanche.'

'Who called you?'

'One of the other three. They were higher than him. The slope broke below them and took him with it.'

Dino strode into the room, zipping up his jacket as he walked. 'Were they carrying transceivers?'

Meg kept her eyes fixed on the map. 'I doubt it.'

'Phone went dead before they could tell me—I'm assuming not.' Sean's face was grim. 'You know how people underestimate the Lake District. Don't any of you do the same. The snow-pack is unstable on the south and north-easterly aspects so this is where we need to be careful. Remember that it's loading—adding weight—that causes most avalanches and the fastest way to load a slope is by wind.'

Still not looking at Dino, Meg pushed her hair under her hat. 'And we've had plenty of wind.'

'Precisely. Wind erodes from the upwind side of an obstacle such as a ridge and it deposits on the downwind side, and wind can deposit snow ten times more rapidly than snow falling from the sky.' Sean sketched a quick picture, showing what he meant. 'Be wary of any slope with recent deposits of wind-drifted snow.'

'So what's the plan?'

'It will take too long to reach them on foot and conditions are clear so, Meg, the air ambulance is going to airlift you, Rambo and Dino straight to the scene. I want you two to work together.'

Great. So much for avoiding him.

Knowing that if she made a fuss she'd just draw attention to herself, Meg gave a nod to acknowledge that she'd heard. Then she kept her head down, preparing herself and Rambo for the challenge ahead. She didn't want to risk looking at Dino in case something showed on her face. If the team sensed that there was something going on between them, she'd never live it down. She was one of the boys. That was the way it was going to stay.

The helicopter dropped them at a safe distance from the base of the gully and Meg immediately put Rambo to work. Lives were at stake. This was no time to be thinking about kissing. Dino apparently felt the same way because he seemed equally focused. Either that or the kiss hadn't affected him the same way it had affected her.

'Can you believe they only have one working mobile phone between the three of them?' Dino scanned the gully. 'You can see where the avalanche started, above that section of wind slab. The others must have been higher up or they all would have been caught.'

'People underestimate these mountains. That's what makes them all the more dangerous.' Meg heard Rambo bark and she pushed herself forward through the deep snow to the bottom of the gully where the dog was already digging.

'He's picked up a scent.' She struggled the final few metres as Rambo carried on digging and barking. 'How long has he been buried? Does he really stand a chance?'

'There's always a chance. Depends how near the surface he is and whether he has space in front of his mouth and nose. Victims often die of suffocation. Off the top of my head I think survival rates drop to about 35 per cent at thirty minutes. On the other hand, friends of mine pulled someone alive from an avalanche in Italy after ten hours, but admittedly that's rare. He was in an air pocket and the weight of the snow hadn't crushed him.'

Dino already had a shovel in his hand and he started to help Rambo. A few minutes later the sleeve of a jacket came into view. Rambo barked and continued to dig. Moments later a man's face appeared, streaked with blood and crusted with snow. He looked at them, dazed, and Meg felt a rush of elation that he was still alive.

'Hang on there. We're going to get you out. Clever boy,' she praised Rambo effusively, and then concentrated on helping Dino dig the last of the snow away.

'I can't feel my feet.' The man was gasping for air and Dino dropped the shovel onto the snow and reached for his backpack.

'That might be the cold, but it's possible that you damaged your back as you fell so we need to be careful as we move you. Can you remember what happened?'

The man screwed his eyes shut, wincing with the pain. 'Visibility was poor, I skied to the far left of the slope. Suddenly my legs went and I was falling. I rolled over and over, couldn't breathe— tried to swim like they tell you to, tried to get my arms up…' He opened his eyes. 'Are my friends safe? They were behind me.'

'They called us before they lost the phone battery. They saw the whole thing but they weren't caught in it. The rest of the mountain rescue team is looking for them now. They were fine when they called.' Meg tried to reassure him while helping Dino carry out the best examination he could in difficult circumstances.

'Does this hurt? Can you feel this?' He was treating the man for head, leg and possible spinal injuries, and Meg used her hands to dig away more of the snow so that Dino had room to see what he was doing.

'Do you want me to contact the search-and-rescue helicopter?'

'Helicopter?' The man groaned. 'I don't think I can get into a helicopter.'

'Trust me, it's the best way. We're going to put you in a vacuum mattress, Dave, to protect your spine,' Dino explained. 'You don't have to do a thing. You'll be winched into the helicopter and they'll get you to hospital.' He nodded to Meg and she quickly made the call while Dino started to prepare the casualty for the transfer.

Dave closed his eyes. 'Can't believe I've been caught in an avalanche in the Lake District. I've walked in the Alps, you know. Can you believe that? This is going to be so embarrassing down at the pub.'

Meg saw Dino's mouth tighten and she knew he was annoyed by that flippant comment.

'You could have died,' she said mildly as she

slipped the phone back into her pocket, 'and so could your friends. The outcome could have been a lot worse than embarrassment.'

'If you've done ski touring in the Alps then you must have carried transceivers? Shovels? Probes?' Dino yanked his equipment out of his backpack and the man looked sheepish.

'In the Alps, yes. I guess we were complacent here.'

'Avalanches eat up complacent skiers and climbers. Don't move, Dave. The winchman is going to lower the vacuum mattress and a stretcher and we're going to get you to hospital.' Dino walked across the snow to find a safe place for the helicopter to land while Meg and Rambo stayed next to the injured skier.

Dave put out a hand to the dog. 'I have you to thank for being found. I recognise that guy. It's Dino Zinetti, isn't it? He used to be a member of the Italian ski team.'

'How do you know that?'

'I'm a keen skier. He was a maniac. His downhill times…' Dave laughed. 'Well, let's just say he isn't really in a position to lecture me for being reckless.'

'He wasn't lecturing. It isn't our job to lecture.'

As the helicopter drew closer, Meg pulled together the rest of her gear, ready to move out. 'But it is our job to point out where additional equipment might have helped so that people don't put themselves in the same position again.' The downdraft from the helicopter flung powdery snow through the air like a blizzard and Meg shifted her position and tried to protect the man from the sudden buffeting of icy wind.

It was only a matter of minutes before Dino came back with the stretcher and the vacuum mattress and together they moved Dave, careful to protect his spine.

'This will hold you secure,' she explained, as they pumped up the mattress and strapped it to the stretcher. 'I expect I'll see you at the hospital. Good luck.'

'Thanks.' The man closed his eyes, choosing not to look as he was winched into the hovering helicopter.

As the aircraft became a dot in the distance, Dino turned to her. 'The team have found the rest of his party on the other side of the ridge, so they're going to walk them back down the other track. We'll go back together. Although frankly this isn't a great place to be walking. There's a lot of loose powder snow up there just waiting to bury someone stupid enough to walk beneath it. Watch yourself.'

Meg glanced up at the pile of snow that had almost claimed a life. 'I have to confess I'm not an expert on avalanches.'

'It isn't hard to spot dangerous slopes when you know what you're looking for.' He drew her to one side and pointed, his breath clouding the air. 'Look up there.'

Trying to block out the fact that he was standing within kissing distance, Meg looked at the snow-covered gully. 'I'm looking.' But it was hard to concentrate. She was breathlessly conscious of him. Unable to help herself, she turned her head and glanced at his profile. It was an unmistake-ably masculine face—eyelashes thick and dark, his jaw shadowed by stubble. Meg felt something elemental uncurl inside her.

'Can you see where the wind slab fractured above him?' His head turned and his gaze sharp-ened as he caught her looking at him.

Meg immediately whipped her head back to-wards the slope, feeling her face turn scarlet. 'Yes,' she croaked, 'I can see.' For a moment she thought she'd got away with it. And then she felt his gloved hand brush against her cheek. He turned her head so that she had no choice but to look at him.

'How long are you going to carry on pretending last night never happened?'

Trapped by his gaze, Meg stared up at him and he slid his hand behind her head and drew her towards him. The blood throbbed in her veins and a delicious, thrilling feeling of inevitability gripped her. As if in slow motion he lowered his head. His eyes held hers until the last moment. And then he claimed her mouth and sent her brain spinning.

Excitement, almost agonising in its intensity, speared her body. Her eyes closed, the world ceased to be grey and white and became a multicoloured kaleidoscope of feelings and emotions. And suddenly there was no doubt left in her head.

Standing in this wild, beautiful place, being kissed by this man, felt completely right. She knew what she wanted. Him. She knew that if he wanted to make love to her here, her answer was going to be yes.

Meg closed her gloved hands on the front of his jacket and leaned into him. His hands were in her hair then on her shoulders and down her back. She tugged at him and he lowered her onto the soft snow, pillowing her head with his arm as he kissed her. And it felt incredible. The skilled brush of his fingers against her face, the warmth of his breath against her mouth as he nudged her lips apart and, finally, the seductive stroke of his tongue as the kiss turned deeper and more explicit.

She'd had no idea, Meg thought dizzily. *No idea that a kiss could feel like this.*

With the snow pressing against her back, she should have felt cold. The air around them was freezing and a few stray flakes had started to fall, but she felt nothing but scorching heat and burning need. Without disconnecting the kiss, Dino drew down the zip of her jacket. Meg gasped as cold air brushed against her flesh and then moaned as he pressed his mouth to the sensitive flesh of her throat. She murmured his name and slid her hands around his neck, her fingers encountering the collar of his jacket as she tried to get closer to him. She wanted to touch—*she needed to feel*—but their outdoor clothing prevented them from anything but the most minimal contact. With a sob of desperation, she twisted against him, feeling the fingers of cold penetrate the neck of her jacket where he'd exposed her flesh. She started to shiver and instantly Dino hauled himself away from her and dragged her to her feet.

'*Mi dispiace*, I'm sorry.' His voice hoarse, he yanked her zip back up to her throat and rubbed her arms to warm her. 'I can't believe I did that. I don't know what I was thinking. You are going to get hypothermia. We shouldn't be doing this here. It isn't the time and it isn't the place.' As if reorienting himself, he glanced around and gave an exasperated shake of his head. 'Can you walk or are you too cold?'

Meg felt numb, but she knew it had nothing to do with the cold and everything to do with the way he made her feel. 'I'm fine. Really.' Or she would be once she'd got herself home and talked some sense into herself. She had a child. She had a life she liked. Why, after all these years, was she risking all that?

Misinterpreting her silence, Dino dragged her against him and held her close, warming her. 'You must be freezing. I can't believe I lost control like that. It's you—the way you make me feel…'

Despite the warning bells in her head, his words

caused a buzz inside her and she pressed her lips to his cold cheek. 'You smell good, have I told you that?'

He turned his head to capture her mouth. 'Unless you want to find yourself flat on your back in the snow again, you'd better not say things like that. All these months I've been feeling as though I need to take a cold shower when you walk into the room, and suddenly I discover that even freezing ice isn't going to work.'

Months?

He'd felt like this for months? She'd had no idea. Seriously unsettled by how much that frank confession disturbed her equilibrium, Meg stooped and picked up a handful of snow. 'Want me to help you out with that problem of yours, macho man?'

Laughing, he caught her wrist in an iron grip. 'Put that anywhere near my trousers and we won't be able to take this any further.'

Did she want to take it further?

Confused by the feelings fluttering inside her, she dropped the snow and stepped close to him. 'Dino—'

He smothered her words with a kiss and then stepped back and held up his hands. '*Accidenti,* enough! We need to get going before we are buried in another avalanche or it grows dark.'

It came as a surprise to realise that she really didn't want to go. She didn't want to leave this place. If he hadn't pulled her to her feet, she never would have stopped. She'd been willing to risk frostbite in order to claw her way closer to him. She hadn't wanted the kiss to end. She would have happily gone on kissing him for the rest of her life, rather than confronting just how dangerous falling under Dino Zinetti's spell could be for her.

Looking around, Meg realised just how isolated they were. The sky was a threatening shade of grey. At some point while they'd been generating heat with each other, it had started snowing again.

Dino hauled his backpack onto his shoulders and secured the waist strap. 'Are you all right to walk?'

Refusing to reveal how shaken she was, Meg gave a mocking smile. 'You may be a good kisser, Zinetti, but even you're not so good I can't put one foot in front of the other.'

'Is that a challenge?' His took her face in his hands and lowered his mouth to hers again. 'Do you know how long I've waited to do this? I was about a day away from just throwing you onto a trolley in the emergency department.' This second frank confession of need made her stomach flip and she laughed against his lips.

'That bad?'

'Worse.' Reluctantly, he lifted his head. 'Much as I'm appreciating the solitude of this place, we have to go. Otherwise our fellow team members will be making another trip up the mountain, this time to rescue us.'

'And that would be almost as embarrassing as being caught in an avalanche in the Lake District.'

Dino helped her slide her arms into her backpack. 'Rambo didn't bark at us. Two bodies in the snow, and he didn't bark. Do you think he knew he was supposed to be discreet?'

'No. He knew we weren't lost.' Meg started to trudge through the snow but it was deep and heavy and the going was exhausting. 'That guy recognised you. Said you used to risk your neck on downhill runs. Why did you stop competitive skiing?' Rambo ran ahead, light on the snow, nosing the ground. She envied his ability to move so easily in the unfriendly terrain.

'I had a couple of injuries. Shoulder…' He flexed his shoulder under his pack. 'That was a nasty one. Concussion. But in the end I just had to make a choice between skiing and medicine. I couldn't compete at high level and study. So instead I combined my mountain knowledge and my medical knowledge.'

'So you must have seen some real avalanches.'

'That was a real avalanche, Meg. And there could be more.' Glancing back over his shoulder to where they'd come from, Dino frowned. 'We ought to talk to Sean about getting some sort of warning issued. Local radio. Hotels. That sort of thing. The snowpack is too unstable for people to be taking risks. In some ways it's even more dangerous than the Alps because people underestimate what they're dealing with here. That man was lucky. It could easily have ended differently and Rambo would have been barking at a dead body.'

Meg shuddered. 'The weather is closing in. Are we going to make it home before dark?'

'Yes. Why? Don't you fancy a night up here in the wilderness with me?'

Struggling with the deep snow, she smiled. 'You

take up too much room in the tent. And anyway, I have to pick Jamie up from my mum's. Tonight is her bridge night or something. I don't want to ruin her social life. Talking of which…' She kept her voice casual. 'I'm afraid I can't make the ball—Ellie needs me to work that shift so I had to swap.'

'Yes, she told me. I swapped it back.' He caught her arm as she stumbled in the deep snow.

'You swapped my shifts?'

'I simply explained to Ellie that you were going to the ball. She was most surprised that you'd offered to switch given that you have a date.'

Trapped, outmanoeuvred, Meg ground her teeth. 'She won't be able to spare me. It's a nightmare trying to staff that shift.'

'On the contrary, she said that given the number of times you've covered for other people over the years, the least she can do is give you the evening off. You're working a late shift. We agreed that you'd work until eight o'clock. The night staff are going to come on early as a favour. It will mean you'll have to get ready at the hospital, but I don't suppose that matters.'

'Now, wait just a minute—'

'Meg.' He locked his hand in the front of her

jacket and pulled her against him, leaving her in no doubt about who was in charge of the decision-making on this particular point. 'Changing your shift isn't going to work. Talking to Ellie isn't going to work. Contracting some mysterious illness isn't going to work. I'm taking you to the ball.'

'What if I tell you I just don't like you enough to go to the ball with you?'

'Then we'll both know you're lying.' Without giving her the opportunity to argue, he leaned in and kissed her. As his lips brushed over hers, her blood heated and for a moment she forgot what they were talking about. Everything important slid out of her mind, leaving a vacant space occupied only by the most intense, sizzling heat she'd ever experienced.

Terrified, Meg shoved at his chest. 'Does that confidence of yours ever get you into trouble?'

'Not so far.'

'You can't run my life.'

'What is it that frightens you? The ball, or me?'

'Both.' Angry with him and suddenly furious with herself too, Meg pulled away from him but he hauled her back against him, his hands firm on her body.

'It's just one evening.' He murmured the words against her lips. 'One evening. If you hate it, I'll take you home after an hour and that's a promise.'

She was about to tell him that an hour was going to seem like a lifetime when she remembered the way she'd felt when he'd tumbled her into the snow. Maybe it wouldn't be so bad. Maybe she should stop being stupid. He was right, wasn't he? It was just a ball and it had been years since she'd been to anything like that. Maybe she'd feel differently about the whole thing now that she was older. It wasn't as if she was going to be standing against the wall, waiting for someone to ask her to dance. She had a partner. And not just any partner—she had Dr Hot.

'All right, I'll go on Saturday,' she said finally. 'If that's really how you want to spend an evening. But don't say I didn't warn you when you come back with bruised feet. You're going to regret this.'

She had a feeling that she would, too.

Rambo sat watching Meg, his tail wagging.

'It's all very well telling me to wear whatever I

have in my wardrobe, but I don't have anything in my wardrobe. One dress. That's it.' Meg pulled it out and hung it on the outside. She brushed the dust off it. Her mother had bought it for her years before when the mountain rescue team had thrown a party to celebrate her eighteenth birthday. Frowning at the plain black dress, she shook her head. She had absolutely no idea what to wear to a Christmas ball, but she knew she wasn't looking at it. She didn't own anything suitable, which meant that now she needed to go shopping and she absolutely *loathed* shopping for clothes. Buying a new pair of hiking boots was easy, but endless rails and racks of different dresses turned her brain to useless mush. She didn't know which colours or styles were in fashion. She didn't know what looked good on her. All she knew was that Dino Zinetti was going to take one look at her and wish he'd never invited her.

Daunted by the prospect of trying to find something to wear, Meg picked up the phone and rang Ellie. 'You're taking me shopping. Since you're the reason I'm going to this stupid ball, the least you can do is help me choose a dress that doesn't make me look awful.'

The fact that Ellie agreed immediately

confirmed Meg's suspicions that her friend and colleague was matchmaking.

They met in the shopping centre a short drive from the hospital.

'This is going to end in tears, you know that, don't you?' Meg scowled as Ellie virtually danced up to her, a smile lighting her whole face.

'It's not going to end in tears.' Ellie slid her arm through Meg's. 'It's going to end in romance. And great sex.'

'Perhaps you should speak a little louder. I don't think those toddlers at the far end of the shopping mall quite heard you.'

'What do you have against sex?'

'El, you're doing it again. A few octaves lower would be good here, otherwise we're going to be kicked out before we've bought anything.'

'Sorry. I'm just so excited that you're going to the ball!'

'That makes one of us.'

'You're not excited? Seriously?'

'I'd rather sing the "Hallelujah Chorus" while standing naked on London Bridge in the rush-hour.'

'Gosh, you are weird.' Ellie bounced up to an

exclusive boutique. 'It's a good job I'm excited enough for both of us.'

Meg took one look at elegant dresses in the window and stepped backwards, narrowly missing a mother with a pushchair. 'If you're even thinking of this shop, forget it. I can't afford it.'

'Look at the sign. Early sale. This is your lucky day.' Ignoring Meg's protests, Ellie tugged her through the revolving glass doors into the daunting hush of the upmarket designer boutique. 'You're going to look perfect. This is going to be a real Cinderella moment.'

'Are we talking about the moment where her clothes fall off or the moment where she loses a shoe?' Meg muttered, but Ellie was already sifting through dresses. Envying her confidence, Meg stood awkwardly, waiting for someone to ask her to leave.

'What colour do you look good in?' Ellie squinted at her and Meg shrugged, hideously embarrassed.

'No idea. My thermal top looks OK on me—that's a sort of emerald green.'

Ellie rolled her eyes. 'Stop talking about thermal tops. On Saturday night you are not Meg, wolf-girl, you are Meg, sex-girl.'

'We are definitely going to be arrested.'

'You should be thinking silk and satin.'

'I'm thinking get me out of this nightmare.' Meg caught the eye of one of the shop assistants. 'Ellie—can we go somewhere more anonymous? We're the only people in this shop and those women are looking at me, wondering what on earth someone like me is doing in here.'

'Rubbish. You're their only customer and they're thinking, I hope she buys something.' Ellie was rifling through the rails. Occasionally she paused and narrowed her eyes before moving on. Finally she pulled a dress out and held it up. 'All right. This is the one. It's stunning.'

'It doesn't have any straps. How does it stay up?'

'It's fitted at the waist and your boobs will keep it up.'

'That's not reassuring. Ellie, I really don't think—'

'Try it. It's really sexy. You could wear your hair up. Do you have a necklace of some sort?'

'No.'

'Well, what do you normally wear around your neck?'

'A wool scarf.'

'I meant when you go out.' Ellie was laughing. 'What do you wear around your neck when you're not trudging through mountains?'

'Nothing.' Meg shrugged awkwardly. 'I don't really wear jewellery. Where would I wear jewellery? If I'm not in the mountains, I'm with my son.' She frowned. 'Actually, I do have something, now I think about it. Mum gave me a gold necklace that used to belong to my grandmother but I've never worn it. It's been in my drawer for seven years.'

'Sounds perfect.' Ellie thrust the dress towards her. 'Try it. Changing room is over there.'

'But—'

'Go. I'll find you some shoes to go with it.'

'Make sure they're flat.' Meg threw an embarrassed glance at the sales girls and gestured to the changing rooms. 'All right if I—?'

They waved her in and she slid into one of the cubicles and closed the door, cursing Ellie for getting her into this mess. It was one of the coldest winters on record and she was about to strip off and try on a strapless dress for an evening she absolutely didn't want to attend. Rolling her eyes, Meg removed her coat and pulled her sweater over her head. Pulling on the dress, she stared at herself sulkily. 'I look stupid.'

Ellie opened the door of the cubicle and looked at her. 'That's because you're wearing boots on your feet. Take them off and try these.' She held out a pair of gold stilettos. 'They'll look really sexy. The dress is completely gorgeous. Meg, no kidding, you look stunning. Is your cleavage real?'

'Of course it's real. You think I got a boob job when no one was looking?' Snappy and irritable, Meg toed off her boots and wriggled her feet into the gold shoes. 'Ouch, ouch, ow! They hurt. Do people seriously wear these things?'

'Yes, because they look fantastic.' Ellie stared down at Meg's feet. 'They also look tight. I'll fetch you a bigger size. Wait there. Don't go anywhere.'

'Trust me, I'm not going anywhere wearing this totally embarrassing dress with these things on my feet. There's half a metre of snow on the ground. I'm going to get frostbite.' Wincing, Meg dragged off the shoes and flexed her toes. 'Why do women do this to themselves?'

Fortunately the next pair Ellie brought her was an improvement. 'How do they feel?'

'As if I'm tipping forwards. I'm going to fall on my face.'

'You just feel like that because you're not used to heels, but you're going to be fine. Now, hair…' Ellie pulled a clip out of her bag and twisted Meg's hair into a knot at the back of her head. 'Looking good.'

'Looking weird.'

'It looks weird because you're just not used to seeing yourself like that. Meg—you're really beautiful. Why do you hate the way you look?'

Meg thought for a moment. 'Actually, I don't hate the way I look. Not really. It's men who hate the way I look.'

'You're talking about one man, Meg, not men in general.' Ellie's voice was tight and there was a flash of anger in her eyes. 'One man didn't like the way you look. And if I ever bump into him I'll break his nose and reposition his features.'

'You won't bump into him. You have two kids and he's allergic to anything remotely domestic.' It pleased her that finally she could talk about him without feeling as though she was going to fall apart. 'Last thing I heard, he was living it up in Ibiza. Dancing on the beach every night with women who spend most of the day getting ready for the night.' The sort of women she'd never understood.

Ellie pulled her into a tight hug. 'With any luck he'll catch some vile disease and his vital organs will drop off. He's history, Meg. It's over and done. And you've protected yourself for long enough. Get out there. Have fun.'

Meg stood frozen in her grasp. 'It isn't fun for me. I can't make people understand that. To me, a ball, a dance, a party—whatever—just isn't fun. It's non-stop stress. Am I wearing the right thing? Is everyone staring? Is everyone laughing at me? The answer to the first is almost always no, and the answer to the second two is almost always yes.'

Ellie sighed and tightened her grip. 'You're as rigid as my cat in a temper. Hug me back. It will make you feel better.'

Knowing when she was beaten, Meg hugged and instantly felt better. Friendship, she thought. Friendship was good. 'For a girl who straightens her hair and wears make-up, you're all right, Ellie.'

'I'm more than all right. And you're going to be more than all right, too. Dino isn't taking you because of your hair or your make-up, Meg. He's taking you because you're *you*. It's you he lo— likes. Remember that.'

Meg pulled away. 'Stop turning this into a big romance. It's one night, that's all. El, this dress is too tight. I can't sit down.'

'It's not tight. It's perfect. And you won't be sitting down, you'll be dancing. Or kissing. I want to be there when Dino first sees you. I know you don't wear much make-up, but this dress needs some make-up.'

'That's the dress's problem, not mine.'

'Do you even own make-up?'

'Of course.' Meg thought about the ancient tubes at the back of the bathroom cabinet. 'Somewhere. Everything has probably dried up by now.'

'If you haven't worn it for years, it will be the wrong make-up. We'll start fresh. Not because you need it, because you don't, but because wearing it will make you feel better.'

An hour later they were sitting in a coffee shop surrounded by bags.

'I honestly can't see myself wearing glitter on my eyes. I'll look like something that fell off the Christmas tree.' Meg poked the foam on her cappuccino. 'And the lipstick is too dark. I look like a vampire.'

'You look great. I'm really excited! I've been dying to see you take a chance on a man.'

'I'm not taking a chance. I'm just going to a Christmas ball, for goodness' sake. We're talking about one date, not a future.'

'Every future starts with one date. You're so wary of everyone, Meg. Matt from Orthopaedics asked you out loads of times, but you said no. Last year it was that really nice doctor from New Zealand whose name escapes me—Pete, that's it. You turned him down too. This is the first time you've said yes. You must really like Dino.'

Meg's palms were damp. Realising that she *did* really like Dino made her want to hyperventilate with panic. How had that happened? *How had she lowered her guard enough to let someone in?*

'Dino?' Her mouth was dry and she struggled to keep her voice casual. 'He's fine.'

'Fine? *Fine?* He's completely, insanely *gorgeous*. Do you know how many of the nurses are trying to get his attention all the time?'

Meg pushed her cup away, feeling slightly sick. 'Yes. Yes, I do know.'

'So you should feel really special. He wants to go with you. He really likes you. You have so much in common. For a start, you both love the mountains.'

'Yes, but being in the mountains is different from being on a date. I'm not worrying about how I look all the time. I'm just me.'

'And it's just you he's invited to the ball,' Ellie said logically. 'So it's no different. It's just that you'll be doing it in a dress. And it's a gorgeous dress. You're going to have a great time. I know you are.'

Meg gave up trying to make Ellie understand. Instead, she shifted the focus of the conversation. 'What are you going to wear?'

'No idea. I have a red dress that I bought before I had the children so if I can still fit into it, I might wear that. Then I have a black one that is good for "fat" days.'

'Wow. More than one dress.' Meg made a joke of it, but deep down she was in full-on panic mode. Maybe she could develop flu. Or maybe her mum could be persuaded not to babysit. Or maybe… With a sigh, she slumped in her chair. It was no good. She was going to have to go.

The whole thing was her worst nightmare.

CHAPTER FIVE

AT LUNCHTIME on the day of the ball, Dino slammed his way through the doors of the emergency department, his bleep sounding and his phone ringing simultaneously. 'Is someone trying to get hold of me?'

'Dino, thank goodness.' Unusually flustered, Ellie pushed equipment into his hands. 'There's a car stuck in snow on the Wrynose Pass. They can't go forwards and they can't go back. You need to go and help. Meg is going with you. I've packed everything I think you'll need.'

'How about a winch?' Dino lifted an eyebrow. 'Since when did we start operating a vehicle recovery service?'

'It's not the vehicle you're recovering, it's the woman inside. She's very pregnant. She was on her way over the pass to stay with her mum, because it's closer to the hospital and she's afraid of being snowed in, but she's now stuck in the snow. Before you say anything, no, it isn't funny.' Ellie stuffed two more blankets into his arms. 'Do you want the rest of the good news?'

'That was good news?'

'This is her second baby. The first one was a precipitate delivery. Thirty minutes from start to finish.'

Dino rolled his eyes. 'In that case, she needs to be airlifted.'

'The helicopter has just been grounded—they've found a fault. They're trying to get another one but in the meantime the only vehicle that can get you up there is the mountain rescue ambulance. Meg's already outside, waiting for you, revving up the engine.'

Dino strode towards the door and flung the extra equipment into the back of the four-wheel-drive vehicle that was used by the mountain rescue team. 'I'm driving.'

'No way.' Meg fastened her seat belt. 'I'm already sitting at the wheel. Get in, macho man.'

'I'll get in when you move into the passenger seat,' Dino drawled, leaning across and undoing her seat belt. 'Move over. I'm not kidding.'

Meg tightened her grip on the wheel and refused to move. 'Chauvinist.'

'Actually, you're wrong. If it were Ben or Sean

sitting in the driver's seat, I'd still move them. I'm Italian. I don't like being driven. Move, Meg, before this woman gives birth in a snowdrift.'

With a sigh, she flounced across into the passenger seat. 'Fine. I'm only doing this because we can't waste any more time. Just don't come squealing to me for help when you've slid off the road because you don't know the bends of the Wrynose Pass. If you're in the wrong gear, you'll never make it.'

'I'll make it.' His hands confident on the wheel, Dino headed along the valley and turned onto the narrow road that led to the beginning of the pass. A snow plough had clearly been along the road before them and the snow was banked high against the stone walls that bordered the fields. 'Why did they pick this route?'

'Because they were desperate and panicking. The forecast for the next few days is really awful. They were afraid that if they waited any longer, they'd be snowed in. One of the disadvantages of living in a remote area.' Meg tucked her hair under her hat and sorted through the equipment. 'Watch yourself on this corner, the road suddenly gets a lot steeper and there's only room for one car. There are passing places, but most of them haven't been cleared since last night's snowfall.'

Dino glanced at her. 'How many times have you driven this road in winter?'

'Plenty. See? You should have let me drive. I know every rabbit hole.' She gave him a cheeky smile. 'The best way to get good at something is to practise. I practised. Driving the mountain passes is one of the best forms of entertainment.'

He was tempted to suggest a few other forms of entertainment that were less life threatening, but he decided this wasn't the time or the place. As they crested the top of the slope, he felt the back wheels of the ambulance slip and heard Meg gasp.

'Relax.' Dino handled the vehicle carefully, feeling the way it responded. 'I'm going to put chains on for the next hill. It's too slick and there's a drop on the right.' He jumped out and fastened the chains to the wheels. The landscape around them had been transformed by the heavy snow and a few abandoned vehicles lay half-buried by the side of the road. It took him less than five minutes to finish the job but that was long enough to freeze his hands.

The snow fell onto the windscreen in big fat

lumps and Dino jumped back into the driver's seat, flicked on the wipers and turned the heating up to full. 'That should improve the grip. It's cold out there.' He flexed his fingers. 'I think the mountain rescue team will be called out tonight.'

'If that happens, we'll miss the ball.' Meg checked her phone for messages and he had a feeling that was exactly what she was hoping would happen.

'I'm flattered to know you're looking forward to our date, *tesoro.*'

'I warned you I wasn't good at that sort of thing. Look, I've said I'll go. What more do you want?'

'Enthusiasm?'

She bit her lip. 'I've bought a dress, so I suppose it would be nice to at least have the chance to wear it.'

'A dress? *Bene.* I look forward to seeing your legs for the first time.' Because he was concentrating on the road, Dino didn't see her frown. 'Is that the car? The red one.'

'Yes, looks like it.' Her voice was strange but when he glanced at her she simply glared at him.

'Keep your eyes on the road or you'll drive off it.' She turned back to look out of the windscreen, narrowing her eyes to see through the falling snow. 'The guy is waving. Why is he waving? He ought to just stay in the warm until we get there. There's no reason to—' She broke off and turned her head slowly. 'Oh, no—do you think…?'

'Possibly, knowing our luck,' Dino gritted, 'but if I drive any faster than this we'll end up in the ditch alongside them. Get on the phone and check on the helicopter situation. Failing that, get the police to meet us at the head of the pass.'

'Any excuse to break the speed limit.'

Dino smiled. 'I'm Italian. That's enough of an excuse.'

While Meg made the necessary calls, he negotiated the switch back turns of the mountain pass and finally pulled up by the red car. Normally it would have been a dangerous place to stop but today, with the world transformed into a white, faceless desert, they were the only people on the road.

'Quickly.' His door was dragged open by the man who had been waving his arms at them. 'Are you the doctor? What the hell took you so long? I'm going to put in a complaint when all this is over. The baby's coming. I'm not kidding. God, you have to do something.' He choked the words out, hyperventilating, and Dino closed his hand over the other man's shoulder, trying to calm him down, choosing to ignore the rudeness.

'Breathe slowly. Deeply. That's better.' He jumped down from the vehicle and found himself in snow up to his knees. The cold immediately clamped his ankles and seeped through his clothing. 'When did her contractions start?'

'About ten minutes ago. I think it's the stress. We never should have left. But I took our little boy to his grandmother's a couple of days ago to give Sue a rest, and Sue was fretting, wanted us all to be together at her mother's for Christmas. If we hadn't left we would have been stranded, and—'

'Hi Mike, it's me.' Meg struggled through the snow and slapped the man on the back. 'Stop panicking. It's all going to be fine, I promise. We just need to get our equipment and then we'll sort her out. Go back and sit with Sue. And stop looking so worried or you'll scare her. Looking at your face is enough to make me go into labour and I'm not even pregnant. Everything is going to be fine.'

The man sucked in two deep breaths and swore. 'It isn't fine, Meg.' His voice was savage and he was clearly on the edge. 'Not every woman is tough. Sue isn't good in cold weather at the best of times. She's delicate and feminine—nothing like you.'

Dino saw Meg's face change.

'Right,' she said tonelessly, 'then we'd better get her out of there, hadn't we? It will be fine, Mike. Trust us.'

'Don't patronise me with all that false reassurance stuff. We're stuck on a mountain pass in the snow and my wife is in labour,' Mike snapped. 'There's nothing fine about it.'

'All right. If I admit we're in trouble, will you stop whining and let us do something about it?' Meg grabbed her bag out of the mountain rescue vehicle and staggered under the weight. 'We're here, and we're good at what we do. Dr Zinetti here has an Olympic gold medal.'

Mike rubbed snow from his face. 'Olympic gold medal? Do they award one of those for delivering babies?'

'Men's downhill, you idiot. Go back to Sue. We'll be with you in a minute.' Meg gave him a push. 'And smile. Tell her everything is going to be OK. We're right behind you.'

As Mike struggled back to the car through the snow, Meg reached into the vehicle for a spare coat. 'What a total idiot. That guy always did have a low burn threshold. Maturity doesn't seem to have improved things.'

'You know him. Is he an ex-boyfriend?' Dino only realised how cold his tone was when she sent him an astonished glance.

'Do you really think I'd hook up with a wimp like him? We went to school together. He was as spineless then as he clearly still is now. The sort who has to have a really, really fragile woman in order to feel big and manly.' She paused, her hand on the strap of her bag. 'What's the matter with you? You look as though you're about to thump someone. What is your problem? I know Mike can be beyond irritating, but you just have to take a breath. To be fair on him, you'd be tense, too, if your wife were about to give birth in a snowdrift.'

Dino fastened his jacket. 'He was rude to you.' *And that had triggered a primitive response far beyond anything he'd experienced before.* 'I didn't like it.'

'I didn't like it much either, but that's life. Some people are rude.' She didn't say anything, but he knew that Mike's nasty comment had hurt her feelings.

Knowing that this wasn't the time or place to deal with it, Dino made a mental note to tackle the subject later.

'So let's check on your friend, Sue. What did the air ambulance say?'

'Still grounded, but paramedics are going to be waiting for us at the head of the pass so we just have to deliver the baby and get them back up this hill.' Surefooted, she picked her way through the deep snow to the car.

'I'm not sure the relevance of telling them about the Olympic gold medal.' Dino used a ski pole to measure the depth of the snow. 'Being able to ski downhill at stupid speeds in tight Lycra isn't much of a qualification for delivering a baby outdoors with a wind chill of minus fifteen.'

'I was trying to impress him. He was one of those sporting jocks at school. Football captain— that sort of thing. Appreciates manly sporting endeavour.' She stopped for a moment to take a breath. 'Winning a gold medal shows grit and determination. A will to succeed and be the best.

Not to mention a certain recklessness that might just come in useful given the situation we're in.'

'I'm never reckless with my patients.'

'Today, you might not have a choice. Come on.' Meg pulled open the car door and slid inside quickly. 'Sue? Fancy bumping into you here— I've been dying to catch up with you for ages, although this wasn't quite what I had in mind.'

Hearing Sue giggle, Dino gave a smile of admiration. No matter who the patient was, Meg always seemed to put them at ease. Even with Mike, she'd managed to control the situation.

Putting his head inside the car, he had his first glimpse of the woman. Short red hair framed a face that was as white as her husband's, and Dino saw instantly that 'delicate' was a fair description. Any thinner and she would have risked being blown away by a gust of wind. Against her slender limbs, her swollen belly looked grossly disproportionate. 'Sue, we need to get you to the ambulance. There's more room and we have better equipment.'

'I can't move. Honestly, I can't move. There's too much pain and I'm scared of the snow. I might slip and that would hurt the baby.'

Dino bit back the comment that being born in a

snowdrift wasn't going to do wonders for the baby either, and tried to give her the reassurance she so clearly needed. 'I won't let you fall, I promise.'

'I really don't—'

'Sue, I've been timing your contractions.' Meg's voice was firm. 'They're coming every two minutes, fast and furious. We really have to move you to the ambulance. We're going to wait until the end of the next contraction and then we're going to get you out of the car and on your feet.'

'I won't get across there before the next contraction starts.' Sue's voice was reed thin and shaky and Mike swore and punched his fist into the seat.

'Can't you see she can't walk? Just get a helicopter or something!'

'She can walk if she does it between contractions.' Meg wrapped an extra coat around Sue's thin shoulders. 'All right. Get ready to swing your legs out of the car. I'm going to help.'

Sue shrank back. 'These boots are new. They're an early Christmas present from Mike. I'm going to ruin them if I walk in the snow.'

Hanging onto his patience with difficulty, Dino exchanged a fleeting glance with Meg. 'I'll carry you.'

Sue's eyes widened and she looked at his shoulders. 'You'll put your back out.'

'No, I won't.' Ignoring Mike's blustering, Dino moved to the car door. 'Slide forward. Put your arms around my neck—that's it.' He swung her into his arms. Checking his footing carefully, he trudged his way through the snow to the four-by-four in less than the two minutes it took for another contraction to start. Meg was already there, opening the doors at the back, and moments later Sue was safely inside what was a comparatively warm place, her new boots dry and untouched by the snow.

Dino tucked blankets around her. 'Keep the doors closed. I'm just going to help Mike secure your car then we're going.'

'I don't think there'll be time.' Groaning in pain, Sue doubled over and Dino slid out of the way and let Meg take his place. He saw her reach for the Doppler probe, ready to listen to the foetal heart.

He heard her say, 'When exactly is this baby due?' and then the only sound was the angry squeal of the wind as it buffeted his body.

He helped Mike clear their belongings out of the car. Piles of brightly wrapped Christmas presents, two suitcases and a hamper of food all needed to be transported to the mountain rescue vehicle and then finally they were ready to leave.

'Baby's heart is one-forty. We all feel better for having heard that. There's a car park just down there on that bend.' Meg leaned forward to talk to him. 'It means going further down the road, but you can turn safely there. There's no way you can turn here, the road just isn't wide enough. You'll go over the edge.'

Sue gave a whimper of fear and Mike's knuckles were white on the seat.

By contrast, Meg's eyes sparkled with the challenge. She was in her element here and Dino suddenly wished they didn't have company in the back of the vehicle.

'You need to be careful when you turn,' she told him, 'otherwise your tyres will spin out and you don't want to lose traction this high up on the pass.'

'All right—tell me where the turning place is.'

It was the most difficult drive of his life and he was relieved Meg knew the road so well.

'Breathe, Sue.' She was in the back with the

labouring woman, encouraging her and keeping her warm.

Dino was just cresting the hill and making the final descent down towards the end of the mountain pass when Sue gave a sharp scream.

'Oh—that's so painful…' She started to sob and Dino pushed his speed as much as he dared.

'I suspect you're in transition, Sue.' He spoke the words over his shoulder, his eyes fixed on the road ahead. 'Meg, you can give her gas and air.'

'One step ahead of you on that one, Dr Zinetti. You just concentrate on the driving. Can you go any faster?'

Not without killing them all. Dino shifted gear and coaxed the vehicle down the final two bends in the road. An ambulance and a police car were waiting.

'Dino.' Meg leaned forward to speak to him. 'There is no way Sue is going to be able to change ambulances.'

'We'll drive her straight to the hospital. With a police escort we can make it in about five minutes.' Dino rolled down his window, had a succinct conversation with the police officer and moments later they were roaring through town behind the police car, sirens blaring and lights flashing.

'It's coming, Meg.' Sue was panting. 'I can feel the head.'

'You have to get her to hospital,' Mike bellowed, his face scarlet as he flapped around in a total panic. 'You have to get her there right now! Aren't you listening to what she's saying? It's coming!'

'I'm listening, Mike, and we don't have to get her to hospital.' Meg's voice was calm. 'If necessary I can deliver a baby here, in the back of our ambulance. No worries. Don't push, Sue. I want you to pant like this…' She demonstrated and Dino smiled to himself.

No worries? Who was she kidding?

Fortunately her confidence seemed to reassure Sue and she was able to relax slightly and control her breathing.

He could hear Meg tearing open a delivery pack and talking quietly to Sue, encouraging her all the time. Somehow she'd managed to block out Mike's pointless ranting and focus on the problem in hand.

Dino pulled up outside the emergency department as close to the entrance as possible. Leaving the engine running for the warmth, he vaulted into the back of the ambulance to help Meg.

'Sterile gloves to your left.' She gestured with her head. 'You're doing so well, Sue. Everything is fine.'

By the time he'd snapped on the sterile gloves the head was crowning. Dino used his left hand to control the escape of the head, murmuring encouragement to the labouring mother.

As the head was delivered, Mike made a strangled noise in his throat and crumpled to the floor of the vehicle with a dull thud.

Sue made a distressed sound and Meg grinned.

'We'll never let him forget that one. He'll be fine, Sue. He's better off staying there until we're done. If we sit him up, he'll just faint again, and at the moment you are our priority. What a fantastic Christmas present—a new baby. You're doing brilliantly. Nearly there. Dino, tell me when to give syntometrine.' She had a syringe in her hand and Dino delivered the anterior shoulder and glanced at her briefly, surprised to see tears in her eyes.

'What? What are you staring at? I like babies. What's wrong with that?' Meg blinked furiously and glared at him, clearly angry that he'd witnessed her emotional response to the situation. 'Do I give this stuff now?'

'*Sì*, now.'

She gave the injection and with a shocked cry Sue delivered the baby into Dino's waiting arms. 'You have a daughter, Sue. Congratulations.' The baby gave a thin wail and he quickly lifted her into Sue's arms. 'Hold her against you. We're going to transfer you to a wheelchair and get you inside because it's too cold out here.'

'A daughter?' The tears started to fall. Tears of relief. Tears of gratitude. Tears of joy. 'I'm going to call her Mary because she was born at Christmas.'

Opening the door of the ambulance, he found a crowd of staff from the obstetric unit waiting to help him and moments later Sue and the baby were inside in the warmth.

Having handed over to his colleagues, Dino returned to the ambulance to find Meg sitting with her arm around a white-faced Mike.

'Actually, I've known several,' she was saying, and she looked up and smiled as Dino approached. 'Just telling Mike he isn't the first father to fall over and bang his head when a baby is born. Everything all right with mother and daughter?'

'The paediatricians are examining Mary, but everything seems fine. In a moment they'll take her up to the postnatal ward.' Dino cleared up the remains of the delivery pack and Mike rubbed a shaky hand over his forehead.

'I can't believe I missed it. It's a little girl?'

'That's right.' Meg jumped down from the vehicle and glanced at her watch. 'I'll take you up there now. Come on. What do you want us to do with all these Christmas presents?'

Mike looked at them blankly, clearly in shock. 'I—I have no idea. Sue's parents are on their way to the hospital now.'

'In which case we can leave the lot just inside the doors with the girls on Reception and you can transfer it all to the car when you're ready.'

Meg closed the door and Mike grabbed her arm. 'Listen—'

'It's OK.' Meg smiled. 'You're welcome.'

Mike looked at her intently. 'You always did have more balls than most men.'

Meg's smile faltered. 'Right. Well—thanks. Have a good Christmas, Mike.'

Looking at her tense shoulders, Dino frowned

and was about to ask her what was wrong when Ellie appeared in the entrance.

'Meg? Can you come? I've just spoken to Ambulance Control and they're bringing in a nasty RTA.'

'Why are people still driving their cars in this weather?' Meg slithered across the icy ground and into the warmth of the emergency department. 'Everyone should just stay at home and watch Christmas TV instead of dicing with death on the roads.'

Ellie looked harassed. 'We're incredibly busy. Dino, can you go straight to Resus? At this rate we're going to be lucky if any of us make it to the ball tonight.'

The rest of the shift was so hectic that Meg didn't even have time to grab a drink. By eight o'clock the emergency department had calmed down a little and it was decided that the staff attending the ball could leave.

Dino glanced at his watch. 'Good job we planned to change at the hospital because there's no time to go home. You have twenty minutes to get ready before the cab arrives. It's never going to be enough, is it?'

Twenty minutes? How long did he think it took a girl to pull on a dress? Meg opened her mouth to tell him that there was no way it would take her anywhere near that long, and then she realised that all the other women he dated probably took three times that length of time to get ready for an evening out with him. He was gorgeous, wasn't he? Any woman spending an evening with a man like him would want to look their best. All the time in the world wasn't going to turn her into the sort of woman he normally dated. Why on earth had she agreed to this? Why was she putting herself through this torture? 'Twenty minutes will be fine,' she said tonelessly, 'I'll do a rush job.'

He gave her a searching look. 'Take as long as you need. I'll drive us. That way it doesn't matter if we're late.'

Yes, it did, because the last thing she wanted to do was make a grand entrance. She wanted to arrive along with everyone else. She wanted to blend into the background. With a shaky laugh at her own expense, Meg hurried towards the staffroom. When had she ever blended at that sort of thing? She was going to stand out like a single poppy in a cornfield.

Ellie was waiting for her in the staffroom.

'Hurry up! I've already heated the tongs. I'm going to straighten your hair before I go and get changed myself.'

Meg flattened herself against the door. 'I was planning to just wear it up like I always do. I prefer it that way.'

'I think you should wear it loose. You have beautiful hair. It's time you showed people how amazing it is.'

Meg allowed herself to waste five of her twenty minutes having her hair straightened. After that it took only a couple of minutes to change into the dress and push her feet into the shoes.

'What are your plans, Ellie? Is Ben picking you up here?'

'He's gone to see someone in the imaging department. I'm meeting him there when I've finished with you. We're going home first, because our house is on the way. Close your eyes while I do your make-up.'

'Don't make me look too made-up.'

'Meg, you're going to the ball. Made-up is good. But I haven't overdone it. You look gorgeous. Just lipstick, then I'm done… There… You can look in the mirror.'

Meg looked. Normally she quite liked her face,

but the make-up seemed to accentuate all the worst aspects of her features. The lipstick made her mouth look too big. The freckles on her nose, earned from so many hours spent outdoors, stood out. Resisting the urge to grab a tissue and rub it all off, she smiled because she didn't want to offend Ellie, who looked genuinely delighted with what she'd achieved. 'Thanks. Wow.'

Ellie's mobile rang and she gasped. 'That's Ben. I need to get going. We'll see you there, Meg. You look fab. Dino is going to be blown away. I wish I could stay to see his face.' She sprinted out of the room, leaving Meg on her own with all her insecurities echoing in her head.

Staring at her reflection, she sighed. She didn't look like herself. She didn't *feel* like herself. Turning sideways, she kept her eyes on the mirror. All right, maybe she didn't look awful. Just weird. Different.

The dress was nice.

Actually, she looked better than she'd thought she would.

Remembering Ellie's comment that Dino would be blown away, Meg picked up the gold clutch bag that Ellie had persuaded her to buy along with the shoes. He wasn't going to be blown away.

She didn't expect that. She didn't have the sort of looks that would turn heads. But she looked OK. Decent. Hopefully he wouldn't be embarrassed to be seen with her.

He'd asked her, she reminded herself firmly. He'd worked with her long enough to know what she was like. He'd kissed her when she'd been dressed in her windproof jacket. She had to look better than she did when she was being blown to bits by a gale.

Meg opened the door of the staffroom and was about to go in search of Dino when she saw him standing in the corridor. He was deep in conversation with a woman wearing a short scarlet dress. It was covered in sequins that sparkled and glinted under the lights.

Short? Meg's stomach plummeted. Was she supposed to have worn something short? Why had no one told her? The invitation had just said 'Black Tie' and she'd interpreted that as meaning that everyone would wear a long dress. Ellie hadn't said anything about the dress being unsuitable. But perhaps Ellie didn't know. As a mother of two young children, she didn't get out much either, did she?

Meg's mouth dried and her heart started to pound.

She looked completely wrong.

Then Meg recognised the woman—Melissa. Staring at her sexy dress, which clung to her body and ended at mid-thigh, Meg wondered why on earth Dino hadn't just invited her to the ball. In all probability he was wishing he had. He certainly seemed to be enjoying the conversation, his laughter echoing down the corridor.

Meg looked down at herself and felt her face burn with embarrassment. It was all too easy to imagine what his reaction would be when he saw her. The comparisons he was going to make. She was going to be a laughing stock. Everyone at the ball was going to be staring at her and feeling sorry for her. *She has no sense of style. No idea how to dress.*

Her palms damp with sweat, Meg closed the door to the staffroom, yanked off the gold shoes and quickly pushed her feet into her trainers.

No way. No way was she putting herself through this. She'd rather fling herself over the edge of a gully, naked. Dino was blocking the only exit, which meant…

Hesitating for only a fraction of a second, she

grabbed her coat and opened the window. The freezing night air poured into the staffroom but Meg didn't care. The cold was the last of her worries. Praying that no one would notice her, she hauled the dress up to her waist, slid nimbly out of the window and moments later she was sprinting through the darkness, the silk dress winding itself around her legs as she fled through the thick snow that covered the grass and on towards the car park. Her feet were soaked in an instant. Twice she tripped and landed on her hands and knees in the snow.

'Stupid, stupid dress.' Her palms stung with pain and she struggled to her feet for the second time and yanked the offending dress up around her waist. Her breath came in great tearing pants and every minute she expected to hear Dino's voice coming from the open window, or footsteps pounding after her. Except that Dino probably wouldn't have bothered following her. He'd probably just think he'd had a lucky escape.

The flash of guilt she felt at having left him standing there with no explanation was eclipsed by the knowledge that she'd done him a favour.

It was only when she realised that she couldn't actually see her car that Meg discovered she was crying. She was so cross with herself. Why, oh, why, had she allowed herself to be talked into going to a ball?

Ellie was wrong. It wasn't fun at all—it was a nightmare. In order for it to be fun, you had to be part of that female club who giggled over the contents of their make-up cases and drooled over dresses, and she did neither of those things. And it was perfectly obvious that Dino was never going to be interested in someone like her. He would have been embarrassed to be seen with her.

She reached her car and pressed her key, some of her panic receding as she heard the reassuring bleep and the clunk as the doors unlocked. Later, she knew, she'd feel guilty. But for now she was just relieved to have made it as far as her car.

Pulling the dress up to her knees so that it didn't get tangled in the pedals, Meg turned on the engine, reversed out of her parking space and accelerated forward.

All right, so Dino seemed to find her attractive, but that was just up on the mountain, when they were working together. Here, doing everyday normal things, she didn't fit and it was no use pretending that she did. She wasn't any of the things he was looking for.

Tears blurred her vision and she brushed them away, struggling to keep her car on the road in the hideous weather conditions.

She contemplated driving to her mother's house, but then decided that would trigger a whole load of questions she didn't want to answer, so instead she took the road that ran along the side of the lake and to her cottage. Her mother wasn't bringing Jamie back until the morning so she had until then to get herself back under control.

Five minutes later she was in the bathroom, scrubbing off the make-up Ellie had so carefully applied, the green dress lying in an abandoned heap on the floor.

She'd just pulled on a cosy bathrobe when she heard the hammering at the door.

Meg froze. Oh, no, no, no. She should have hidden the car. She should have turned off all the lights. She should have—

'Meg! *Maledezione.*' Anger thickened his accent. 'Open this door right now!'

She didn't move. Had he come here just to shout at her? Probably. She deserved it, didn't she? She'd left him standing there. He was a senior consultant and people were expecting him to attend the ball. Because of her, he wasn't going. Because of her, everyone would be talking.

Braced for him to hammer on the door again, she almost died of shock when she heard the sound of a key in the door. Before she could move, he was at the top of the stairs.

Meg took one look at the thunderous expression on his face and flattened herself against the door of the bedroom. 'Where did you get a key to my house?'

Dressed in a black dinner jacket that shrieked of expensive Italian tailoring, he looked sensational. And furious.

Guilt ripped through her. 'Go ahead, yell at me. I know I deserve it. I know I behaved like a coward and I'm prepared to take what's coming to me. Just do it. Get it over with and then you can leave. You're all dressed up and it probably isn't too late for you to find a woman you'd like to take.'

'*You* are the woman I wanted to take! But you climbed out of a window and ran across two flower beds.' He ran his hand over the back of his neck, his handsome face a mask of incredulity and disbelief. 'What is going on? *What is the matter with you?*'

Her heart was hammering against her ribcage. 'Where did you get a key to my house?'

'Your mother. It was the first place I looked for you.'

'Then you wasted your time because I'm not going.'

'I didn't look for you in order to force you to come,' he gritted. 'I looked for you because I was worried.'

Thinking about the lecture she was now facing from her mother, Meg made a sound that was halfway between a sob and a laugh. 'She had no right to give you the key to my house. She had no right to interfere.'

'She's trying to stop you sabotaging every relationship.' Dino loosened his bow tie with impatient fingers. '*Why* are you sabotaging it, Meg? Explain. Is this to do with Jamie's father? Or is it that you don't like my company?' When she didn't answer he took a deep breath and tried again. 'There are banks and safety deposit boxes that are easier to break into than you. Do yourself a favour and drop the self-protection for a few minutes. I'm trying to understand you.' He undid the first few buttons of his shirt and she wondered if he were doing it on purpose to make things harder for her. Was he trying to remind her about their chemistry?

'You know I like your company,' she croaked. 'It isn't that.'

'Then what is going on?'

She'd hurt his feelings. She was a bad person. 'I don't blame you for being angry but I honestly don't know why you would *be* this angry because it can't possibly matter to you that much.'

'I'm *not* angry,' he breathed, 'at least, not with you. If you want to know the truth, I'm furious with myself for not taking notice when you said you didn't want to go to the ball. Instead of pushing you, I should have asked you why.'

Her heart skittered and jumped. 'You're not angry with me?'

'Exasperated, yes. Puzzled, definitely. Angry? No. How could I be angry? You must be extremely traumatised to be prepared to launch yourself out of the window into a snowdrift to escape me. Am I that scary?'

'Not you. I wasn't escaping you. I was escaping the evening.'

He looked at her and shook his head. 'Are you going to explain any of this to me?'

Meg dragged her gaze away from the bronzed

skin at the base of his throat. He deserved an explanation, didn't he? That was the least she could do after leaving him standing. She took a deep breath, trying to stay calm as she spoke of the past she'd tried so hard to forget. 'The night Hayden told me he was involved with another woman…' It was an effort to force the words through the barriers she'd erected. '…we were supposed to be going to a ball. I'd just told him I was pregnant and he thought it was important that I know right away we didn't have a future. That he didn't want to keep up our relationship. He said that I was wrong for him. That he didn't want to be with someone like me.' Her voice thickened and she cleared her throat, desperately choking back tears. 'Someone who was more at home in the mountains than a nightclub. He said I just wasn't glamorous enough for him.'

'Hayden is Jamie's father?'

Meg's voice hardened. 'Well, that sort of depends on your definition of father. Given that he's never actually seen Jamie, I wouldn't exactly say he ever really earned himself the title of father.'

'Right. So we've ascertained he's emotionally impaired, intellectually challenged and monumentally selfish. Did anyone ever diagnose his visual problem?'

'Visual problem?' She stared at him in confusion

'You're beautiful, Meg.' Dino stood strong and firm in front of her, not budging an inch. 'Really beautiful. If he couldn't see that, he obviously had a visual problem. Myopia? Cataracts?'

'He just had a thing for well-groomed women. And who can blame him?' She lifted her head and looked at him, forcing herself to meet his eyes as she revealed the most humiliating part of it all. 'Do you know the thing that hurt most? The night he told me I wasn't glamorous enough, I'd really made an effort. He'd wanted to go to this stupid ball and I'd decided that I ought to support him, so I spent ages on my hair and face and I thought I looked good. Until he said that. And just to make sure I knew how far short of the competition I was, he'd brought my replacement in the car with him.' Meg's knees shook slightly as she remembered the horror of that moment. 'She was sitting outside the whole time he broke up with me. He took her to the ball instead. I haven't been to one since. I decided to stop trying to be something I wasn't.'

'Meg—'

'I'm sorry I messed up tonight. I'm sorry I embarrassed you,' she croaked. 'When it comes to social stuff, I'm a coward. And that is why this is never going to work between us and why you should just turn right around and walk back out of that door. Because if we carry on with this relationship, I'll just do it to you again. And then you'll hate me.'

'*When* we carry on with this relationship, I'll make sure you don't do it to me again and I'm certainly not going to hate you.'

His words terrified her. 'You need a woman who isn't afraid to dress up and stand by your side. The truth is, we're colleagues. You're a fantastic doctor and you've got a killer smile and you just happen to kiss like a sex god, but none of that is going to make this work.'

'Colleagues? A few days ago we almost had sex in the snow. Call me old-fashioned, but I don't normally behave like that with a "colleague".'

'That was a one-off, probably triggered by the intense adrenaline rush of the avalanche threat.'

'If it was a "one off", how do you explain the kiss in your kitchen? We have a relationship, Meg.' He closed his hands over her shoulders, his grip firm and possessive. 'No matter how determined you are to fight it. Answer me one more question—despite the way you felt, you obviously did intend to come to the ball tonight. Why did you change your mind?'

'Because I got it wrong again.'

'What did you get wrong?' Dino frowned. 'You mean the way you dressed?' His eyes narrowed and he turned his head to look through the open door into the bathroom. Muttering under his breath in Italian, he strode into the room she'd just vacated and picked up the dress from the floor. 'You were wearing this tonight? This was the dress you chose for the ball?'

Knowing exactly what he was thinking, Meg felt her face turn scarlet. 'Yes. Sorry. I didn't know.'

'Didn't know what?'

'That we were supposed to wear short dresses,' she blurted out. 'That's why I don't go to these things, Dino. I avoid them for exactly that reason. Hayden was completely right that I don't have a clue! I never know what to wear, or what bag to carry, or w-what height of heel I'm supposed to pick—I don't know anything.' Her voice rose. 'I'm rubbish at that sort of thing. Completely, totally useless. Always have been. When other girls were playing with Barbie dolls, I was learning to fit crampons to my boots. You heard Mike. He told me I had bigger balls than a man! He told me that Sue was delicate, whereas I'm not. No one worries about me ploughing through snow because I'm as strong as a horse.'

'I wouldn't want to be with a woman like Sue,' Dino gritted. 'She would drive me mad and I would very probably want to kill her within two minutes, which isn't a good basis for a long-term partnership.'

'Stop being nice to me. It's making me feel even more guilty.' Meg rubbed the palm of her hand over her face and noticed black on her fingers. 'You see? This is why I don't wear make-up— now I have mascara everywhere and I probably look like a panda.'

He grabbed a towel from the bathroom and gently wiped her face. 'You don't look like a panda.' His gentleness was the final straw and the last of her control crumbled.

'I'm sorry I left you standing there. I never should have said I'd go with you. I'm a truly horrible person and I feel really bad. I wish you'd just shout and rant.' She gave a hiccough. 'And now

I'd be really grateful if you'd go away and leave me alone. I need to hide under the duvet.'

But he didn't let her go. Instead, he folded her into his arms and hugged her tightly. 'You saw me talking to Melissa, didn't you? She caught me just as I was about to come and get you. You saw Melissa and that's when you turned and ran.'

Crushed against hard male muscle, Meg felt her limbs melt. 'You should have taken her.' He smelt so good. *He felt so good.*

'I didn't want to take her. And your dress was perfect, *tesoro.*' His voice was husky. 'I just wish I'd seen you wearing it. You should have walked out of that room with your head held high and I would have been proud to have you as my date.'

'Not when you saw how I stacked up against everyone else. Everyone would have been staring at me. And feeling sorry for you.'

'If they stared it would have been because you are beautiful, not because you were dressed inappropriately. And if they felt anything for me, it would have been envy. You shouldn't be insecure about the way you look.'

'I'm not insecure. I like the way I look.' Meg sniffed and pulled away, noticing black smudges on his shirt. 'It's just that the way I look doesn't suit all that social stuff. I like wearing walking boots and tramping through the mountains, I just don't like wearing dresses and putting on make-up. I haven't got the right sort of face or body for that.'

'You have a beautiful face and a woman's body,' Dino drawled, 'and even though I think you look seriously cute in your walking gear, it would be a novelty to see your legs once in a while.'

'Why? Honestly, why are you bothering?' Her throat was clogged with tears. 'All right—yes, I saw Melissa this evening. I thought she looked gorgeous. She looked sexy and feminine—every-thing I'm not. I'm wolf-girl, Dino, and putting a dress on me doesn't change that. Even if I'd worn Melissa's dress, I still wouldn't have looked as good as she did. I'm just not a girly girl. I'm the person who can manoeuvre a car out of a snow-drift, but I can't apply mascara. You heard what Jamie said—I'm just not that feminine.'

'Really?' His eyes glittering dark, he slid the robe off her shoulders and Meg gasped and made an abortive grab for it.

'What are you doing?'

'You told me you're not that feminine. I prefer to make my own decisions about these things.'

He trailed a leisurely hand over the curve of her hip. 'Sorry, but I'm going to have to disagree with you.'

Meg made another grab for her robe. 'Dino, please…' Scarlet with embarrassment, she tried to cover herself but he dropped it on the floor behind him.

'You think I care what dress you're wearing? You think that's why I want you? So how do you explain the fact that I wanted to strip you naked when you were wrapped up in layers of thermal insulation on the mountain?' The heat of his mouth was a breath away from hers and she could feel hard muscle through the thin fabric of his shirt. 'You think I'm interested in the way you wear your hair?'

Transfixed by the look in his eyes, Meg felt the room spin. 'Dino—'

'Just for the record, I don't care about any of that.' He backed her against the door in a purposeful movement. 'I care about the woman underneath. If you want the honest truth, there is nothing sexier than a sleek, athletic body, and yours is the best I've ever seen. Is this your bedroom?'

Her heart hammering, Meg nodded and he swept

her up, strode into the bedroom and deposited her in the centre of the bed. Then he threw off his jacket and came down on top of her, pinning her arms above her head so that she couldn't wriggle away. Stretching out his free arm, he flicked on the lamp by the bed and a soft golden light spread across the room.

Mortified, Meg twisted under him. 'Let me go. I'm going to punch you in a minute.'

'Then there's no incentive to let you go, *tesoro*.' His sensual mouth curved into a devastating smile. 'I have you captive. No more running. No more avoidance tactics. For tonight, you're mine.'

'At least turn the light off.'

'No. How can you not know you're beautiful? You have an incredible body and working alongside you for so long has been driving me crazy.' He lowered his mouth to her neck. Licked at the sensitive spot below her ear. 'What are you scared of, Meg? Why are you always pushing me away?'

Her body was quivering. 'Because that's what I do. Because you're going to hurt me and then you're going to hurt Jamie and I'm not going to let you.'

He lifted his head, his eyes deadly serious.

'Let's get one thing straight.' He took her face in his hand, forcing her to look at him. 'I'm not going to hurt your son, Meg. That's just not going to happen.'

'But if—'

'It is *not* going to happen.'

Which meant what, exactly? She tried to work it out but he was kissing her again and suddenly her brain was too fuzzy to make the necessary connections. Meg writhed underneath him but he didn't budge. He just kissed her until she thought her brain was going to explode—until her body was shrieking with a need that only he could satisfy, and all the time his clever fingers touched, caressed, explored. 'Don't do that.' Her voice was a soft plea. 'Damn you, you're not playing fair.'

Ignoring her, he trailed his mouth down her neck and lingered on the swell of one breast. 'Who said anything about fair? We stopped playing fair when you decided to run from me without explanation.' He closed his mouth over the peak of her nipple and Meg felt an explosion of sexual excitement spear her body.

'Don't—please.' She gasped the words. 'When you do that I can't...'

'You can't what? You can't resist me? You can't

think straight?' Dino lifted his head and looked at her from under lowered lids, his eyes glittering in the dim light. 'Good. Because that's how I feel about you. By the time I've finished with you, you're going to be in no doubt that you're a woman. It doesn't matter how you're dressed, Meg. In fact, clothes are an irritation if I'm honest. I just want to strip you naked.'

Meg felt as weak as a newborn kitten. She knew she should push him away, but her body and brain appeared to be disconnected. As he tortured her with fingers, lips and tongue, she lost contact with the part of her brain responsible for decision-making. She wriggled and writhed underneath him, driven wild by his skilled touch. Her head swam, her body trembled, and when he brought his mouth back down on hers, she felt as though she'd lost her mind. Hot, hard and demanding, he took her mouth in a searing kiss that left her in no doubt as to how their evening was going to end. It was crazy and desperate, his tongue meeting hers in a skilled, knowing assault that was shattering in its intensity. When he dragged his mouth from hers, she moaned a protest and locked her hands behind his head.

'Don't stop. You can't stop. You started this…'

'And I'm going to finish it. I love your hair,' he breathed, sliding his fingers through the silky mass, 'I love your hair loose like this—that night after we rescued Harry, that was the first time I'd ever seen you with your hair down. Every day since then I've wanted to see it again. Can you feel what you do to me?'

He moved her hand down his body and Meg felt her heart leap and her mouth dried as she touched him intimately.

Oh, yes, she could feel.

She could feel the throbbing heat of him against her—could feel the power and size of him. And she knew he could feel what he did to her because his fingers were touching her, skilfully exploring the hot, moist core of her body, and it felt so unbelievably good that Meg gave a moan of disbelief. It felt as though she was being burned at the stake, her body devoured by a dangerous cocktail of sexual heat and wicked anticipation, the throb in her pelvis almost agonising in its intensity.

Finally, when she was ready to beg, he pulled away from her, but it was only a brief pause before he came back over her, his eyes glittering dark as he lifted her hips.

'Look at me!' His voice was thickened by raw passion. 'I want you to look at me. I want you to know it's me.'

'I know it's you, Dino.' With difficulty, she galvanised her dazed brain and looked. And looking added another dimension to the whole sensual feast because his eyes blazed almost black with a raw passion that threatened to explode out of control.

Beyond the windows, a thick layer of snow covered the ground but here, in the intimate atmosphere of her bedroom, scorching heat simmered between them. The outside world had ceased to exist.

Meg felt him, hot and hard against her, and then he was inside her, entering her with a series of slow, purposeful thrusts that took him deep. For a moment she didn't dare breathe, and then a wild rush of excitement shot through her and she wrapped her arms around him tightly, feeling him with every nerve ending and fibre of her body. He was still wearing his shirt and she tore at the last of the buttons, frantic to touch him, desperate to run her hands over the satin-smooth muscle of his shoulders.

He murmured something in Italian and then

thrust deeper, his body sinking into her tender, sensitised flesh, and Meg went up in flames. Scorching, explosive excitement engulfed her and he started to move, each skilled stroke designed to drag the maximum response from her. His shirt hung loose and she sank her fingers into the sleek muscle of his hard shoulders, completely out of her mind with the pleasure he created.

It was wild and out of control, her teeth on his shoulder, his hand in her hair as he drove into her, sending them both rocketing skywards. Meg felt her body shatter into a million sparkling pieces and she heard him groan her name as he hit the same peak. His mouth came down on hers again and they kissed all the way through it, the erotic stroke of his tongue adding to the intensity of the moment.

It had to end, because nothing so intense could possibly last. Meg felt him shift his weight from her, his breathing unsteady as he rolled onto his back and covered his face with his forearm.

Feeling nothing like herself, Meg stared blankly at the ceiling. She could have told herself that she'd reacted in such a wild way because she hadn't had sex for so long, but she knew that wasn't true. The truth was, she'd reacted in such a wild way because Dino drove her wild. He was the sexiest, hottest man she'd ever met and when she was with him her body had a will of its own. She'd wanted him so badly she hadn't thought about anything else.

Slowly, he turned his head to look at her. '*Mi dispiace, tesoro*—sorry.' His voice was husky, his tone holding a mixture of apology and amusement. 'I had hoped for a little more finesse than that. But I have wanted to get you naked for such a long time, my control was seriously challenged.'

He'd wanted her that badly?

Not for anything would she admit how flattering it was that a man had wanted her so badly he hadn't even bothered undressing. He lay next to her, his shirt undone to the waist, exposing a powerful chest and hard, defined stomach muscles. 'You're not even undressed.'

'I was in a hurry,' he purred, 'but any time you want to do something about that, just go ahead.' He locked his hands behind his head, his eyes challenging her.

Meg swallowed. 'I really am sorry I ruined your evening.'

He gave a slow, satisfied smile. 'My evening

turned out extremely well, *tesoro*. How was yours?'

Blushing, she snuggled against him, resting her head on his shoulder. 'Not bad.'

'Not bad? *Not bad?*' Laughing, he rolled her onto her back. 'Then I'd better try again, because I want a lot more from you than "not bad".'

He kissed his way down her body, ignoring Meg's gasp of shock.

'Honestly, Dino, you can't...'

But he did. And when she was pliant and trembling, he rolled onto his back and lifted her so that she straddled him. Her hair flopped forwards, brushing his chest, and this time he entered slowly, his hands hard on her hips as he filled her. His eyes never leaving hers, he made it the most intimate experience of her life. She saw the faint sheen of sweat on his brow and the tension in his powerful shoulders. And then he started to move inside her and she closed her eyes as she felt her body accommodate the whole silken length of him. And nothing had ever felt more right. It was all about the moment. Not the past, or the future, just this one moment.

'*Belissima*. You're beautiful,' he said thickly, his dark eyes hot. 'You feel incredible.'

'So do you.' She gasped the words and then leaned forward and kissed him, her hips matching the perfect rhythm he set.

He groaned her name and tightened his grip on her hips. 'Slow down, *tesoro,* or I'll—'

'You'll what?' Feeling her feminine power, Meg smiled and licked at his mouth. 'You'll what? Struggling to hang onto control, macho man? Have you got a bit of a problem there?'

His jaw hard and set, he muttered a curse and drove into her hard, and her ability to tease him evaporated in the sudden heat of their passion. She couldn't speak or think. As he hit his peak she felt her body do the same, convulsing around the thrusting length of him and exploding into the heavens.

CHAPTER SIX

'MUM? *Mum!*'

'Oh no!' Waking in a panic, Meg shot out of bed, her heart hammering. Light peeped through a gap in the curtains and she grabbed the clock and tried to focus on the numbers. 'It's nine o'clock? Dino, we overslept. I didn't mean you to stay the whole night. Jamie's home! You have to go. Quickly! Oh, why didn't I set the alarm? I'll take them into the kitchen and you sneak out the front door.' Flustered and panicking, she grabbed the first thing she could find, which just happened to be a pair of ancient jeans she'd worn the day before to clean the bathroom. Thrusting her arms into a jumper, she freed her hair and turned to look at him.

It was a mistake.

He was six feet two of sleepy, gorgeous man. The sight of his powerful shoulders and shadowed jaw was enough to make her want to leap straight back in to bed again. He had to be the sexiest man alive.

'Mum?'

'Dino, move!' In desperation, Meg threw his dress shirt at Dino, forcing her mind from sex to motherhood. It was an uncomfortable and unfamiliar transition. 'Put something on, quickly. I'm so cross with myself...' Shaking, she pushed herself into her trainers. 'We shouldn't have done this. I don't want to hurt Jamie.'

'*Calma, tesoro.* Calm down. No one is going to hurt Jamie.' His voice still husky from sleep, Dino swung his legs out of the bed and she had a brief glimpse of wide shoulders and rippling pectoral muscles before he shrugged on the shirt she'd thrown him.

It was impossible not to notice that he was aroused and Meg gave a gulp. 'Dino...'

'It will be fine now you're not walking around naked.' A wry smile touched his mouth as he intercepted her glance. 'Go to your son, Meg, before he comes to you.'

For a second their eyes held and, in that single breathless moment, Meg felt something shift inside her. Whatever they'd shared in the darkness of the winter night hadn't gone. It was still there. And it felt good. *And confusing.*

Her head in a spin, she turned and shot out of the room, closing the door firmly behind her just as Jamie came thundering up the stairs. 'Hi, sweetheart! Did you have fun at Grandma's house?' *Did she look as though she'd spent the night having sex?*

No, of course not.

As far as Jamie was concerned, she'd spent the night alone.

'Hi, Mum.' Snowflakes dusted his coat and his cheeks were pink from the cold. 'Where's Dino?'

Or maybe not.

Meg tightened her grip on the door handle. *So much for sneaking him out of the house.* 'Wh-why are you asking? What makes you think that Dino—?'

'His car is parked outside the front door.' Jamie bounced up to her and hugged her round the waist. 'Did he do a sleepover? I'm really sad I missed it.'

'Yes, he did a sleepover. He had to do a sleepover because he…er…he…well, it really doesn't matter. Tell me what you did with Grandma. Did you wrap presents?' Meg swung Jamie up into her arms before he could charge into the bedroom and carried him back down to the kitchen. 'You're getting too heavy for me.'

'I'm going to get even heavier because Grandma is making us pancakes.'

Which meant her mother wasn't planning on leaving any time soon. Feeling as though she was facing a firing squad, Meg walked into the kitchen. Hoping Dino would take the chance to escape, she closed the door behind her.

Moments later it opened and Dino walked in.

Ignoring Meg's appalled glare, he ran his hands through his ruffled hair and smiled at her mother, who was assembling the ingredients for pancakes. '*Buongiorno*. I must apologise for my appearance but I wasn't planning on staying the night.'

Meg's mouth fell open and she caught a glimpse of her mother's smug smile before Jamie threw himself at Dino. 'You had a sleepover.'

'*Sì*, a sleepover.' Dino swung the boy into his arms and smiled at him while Meg watched, her heart in her mouth. His jaw was dark with stubble and eyes had the same sexy, dark brooding quality that had seduced her out of her knickers the night before. And seeing him with her child made her feel…

Vulnerable.

It wasn't just about her, was it? It was about so much more than her. He'd promised not to hurt her child, but no one could make a promise like that, could they? He wasn't even Jamie's father. Not that you'd know that by looking at the two of them together.

Jamie was clinging, his arms locked around Dino's neck like bindweed. 'I didn't know you were doing a sleepover.'

'I'm afraid the Batmobile let me down. Really she is a warm-weather car. You know that. She has a high-performance engine and that makes her very temperamental. She loves the warm weather, but I insist on driving her in the winter so occasionally she punishes me by refusing to start. All that snow yesterday upset her. I was stranded here. Your mum kindly let me stay.'

Impressed by his impromptu excuse, Meg relaxed and then spotted the sceptical look on her mother's face. The excuse might work on Jamie, but it wasn't going to work on Catherine Miller. She was a much tougher audience to convince.

Jamie bounced in Dino's arms. 'Wow—so now

you're here you might as well stay the whole day. Sundays are my favourite day because we have pancakes for breakfast. Say you'll stay—*please*. Do you like pancakes? I have them with maple syrup and chocolate.'

Dino winced. 'Together?'

'Yup, that's how I like them. And then we're going to buy our Christmas tree. You could come.' Jamie held his breath and so did Meg because she couldn't bear to see his disappointment. And she knew that he was going to be disappointed. There was no way Dino would want to spend the day choosing Christmas trees, was there?

Her lower lip clamped between her teeth, Meg waited for Dino to deliver a smooth excuse, but instead he nodded. 'Thanks for inviting me, I'd love to come. As long as we call in at my house on the way so that I can change my clothes. I can't choose a Christmas tree wearing a bow-tie.'

'I could lend you something…' Jamie looked at his shoulders doubtfully '…but I don't think I have anything that would fit you. You look like a real live Superhero.' He squeezed Dino's shoulders with his hand, completely unselfconscious. 'How do you get muscles like that? I want to have muscles. I want a six-pack. I do sit-ups, but so far I haven't even got a two-pack. Will you show me how?'

Dino grinned and lowered him to the floor. 'I think you might have to wait a few years for a two-pack. When the time comes, I'll show you how. Meg, can I use your bathroom for a shower?'

The thought of him in her shower sent the colour flooding into her cheeks. 'Of course.' Her mind was in a spin as she attempted to decipher what was going on. Why had he agreed to spend the day with them?

Displaying none of her reticence, Jamie grabbed his hand. 'I'll show you where the bathroom is. Do you need a towel? You can borrow one of mine. Would you prefer Superman or The Incredible Hulk? Did you bring a sleeping bag for your sleepover?'

Meg watched them, man and boy, her heart twisting as she saw hero-worship and trust in her son's eyes. This is what it should have been like. How it should have been for Jamie. Didn't every child have a right to that?

Part of her wanted to reach out and hug him close—warn him that trusting came with a high price. But another part of her—a small part—

wanted to walk further down the path and see where it led.

As the door closed behind them, her mother handed her a cup of coffee. 'Jamie really likes him. Relax.'

'The fact that Jamie really likes him is the reason I can't relax. Jamie is so trusting. He just doesn't see bad in anyone. I'm afraid...' Meg curled her hands around the mug. 'I'm afraid he's going to get hurt. How far do I let this go? How close should I let him get?'

'You can't protect him from everything.'

'No, but I can try.' And by allowing Dino into her life she was risking not just her own happiness, but Jamie's. When Dino decided that he'd had enough of her, it wouldn't just be her that suffered, would it?

Her mother measured out flour and added it to a bowl. 'I know what you're thinking, and you're wrong. Sometimes, Meg, you need to take big strides through life, even if that means falling over. You fell, hard. And now you need to get up again. You need to be brave.'

Meg was affronted. 'I am brave.'

'Yes, when you're walking through a blizzard, or hanging off the end of a rope. But then you've never been scared of the physical stuff. If it doesn't frighten you then it isn't brave. And what frightens you is the emotional stuff.' Catherine added eggs to the flour and whisked. 'I'm glad he stayed the night.'

'I didn't plan that. But you gave him a key so he barged his way in.'

'Good. You can thank me any time you like. I'm not sorry about that. I am sorry we caught you unawares. I should have thought of that and phoned first.'

'Nothing happened, Mum.' Horribly uncomfortable, Meg pushed her hair out of her eyes. 'He slept in Jamie's room.'

'Meg, I may be old but I'm not stupid. And neither are you. If you let that man sleep in Jamie's room then you are even more of a desperate case than I think you are.' Her mother gave a tiny smile. 'Really, you don't have to lie to me. I know I'm your mother, but frankly I'm delighted that you've finally had sex. Looking at Dino, I have every confidence that it was excellent sex. I'm thrilled to see you finally letting your guard down. Can you pass me some milk from the fridge?'

Meg dragged open the fridge door and stood for

a moment, hoping that the cool air would reduce the heat of her face. 'I don't want him to come and get the Christmas tree with us.'

'Why not?'

'Because it's a family trip. Our routine.' She closed the fridge door and handed her mother the milk. It was impossible to contain her fears. 'And because he's just being polite. I'm sure the last thing he wants is to spend the day with us.'

'You don't know that. He doesn't strike me as a man who has a problem with decision-making. If he didn't want to come, he would have told you. I think you're spending too long second-guessing him. Sometimes you just have to take people at face value.'

'I did that once before, remember?'

'Yes, I remember.' Catherine poured milk slowly into the batter mixture, whisking all the time. 'But you can't let that one episode of bad judgement affect all your life choices.'

Meg frowned. 'You think Hayden was bad judgement?'

'Appalling judgement. It was completely obvious that he was shallow, selfish and totally focused on himself.'

'It was obvious?'

'Right from the first day.'

Meg scowled. 'But you didn't think to mention it?'

'You were nineteen. Would you have listened if I'd mentioned it?'

'Probably not.' Meg put her coffee down on the table in a huff. 'But given I'm so much older and wiser now, perhaps you'd better tell me now what you think about Dino.'

'I think he's clever, good looking, responsible, strong...' Her mother whisked skilfully. 'Sexy, of course, but I'm sure even you can see that bit without me pointing it out.'

'So he's Mr Perfect.' But her mother was impervious to Meg's sarcasm.

'No. There are shadows there. Scars.' Her mother frowned. 'He's led a real life. A life with ups and downs and traumas. A life like any other. But he's man enough to face those things head on and deal with them. Learn from them. He's not the sort to run from anything awkward or difficult.'

Meg gaped at her. 'How long have you spent with him?'

'I don't need long. It's one of the advantages of getting on in years. You have plenty of past data to draw on. Can you rinse some blueberries?

Dino didn't look too excited at the combination of maple syrup and chocolate. The least we can do is feed him something he enjoys.'

'Mum, I don't have any blueberries! I don't have anything in my fridge except the basics, you know that. I know how to cook food a seven-year-old likes. Spaghetti. Meatballs. Chicken in breadcrumbs.' Meg's mood dropped even further. Good sex wasn't enough to sustain a relationship, was it? 'If the way to a man's heart is through his stomach, I'm doomed.'

'Well, let's hope Dino likes chicken in bread-crumbs. Just remember to throw out mouldy cheese. There are blueberries in the basket by the door. I brought them with me. And a Christmas cake that I iced for you.'

'Thanks.' Her mind in turmoil, Meg smiled absently. 'Jamie will love that.'

There was a pause while her mother put the bowl to one side. 'Why didn't you go to the ball?'

Meg dug through her mother's basket and retrieved the fruit and the cake. 'I don't want to talk about that.'

'I was very surprised to see Dino at my door.'

Guilt squirmed in her stomach. 'I'll pay for the tickets.'

'I don't think he was worrying about the money.' Her mother rinsed the blueberries and tipped them into a bowl. 'He was worried about you. He likes you, Meg.'

Meg thought about the night before—*about the passion they'd shared.* 'Maybe.'

And she liked him. Which made the whole thing all the more terrifying.

'Why not let the relationship take its course?'

'Because when it crashes to the ground, I don't want Jamie caught in the rubble.' Meg broke off as Jamie bounded back into the room, Rambo at his heels.

'Dino didn't actually need any help, so I let him shower on his own.' He climbed onto a chair and helped himself to a handful of blueberries. 'He's going to go with us to buy a tree. Isn't that cool?'

Was it cool? Meg wasn't sure what she thought about it except that the whole situation was an explosion waiting to happen.

She felt as though she was free-climbing, clinging to a vertical rock face without the support of a rope.

How far was she going to fall?

* * *

'This is your house? Wow.' Jamie slid out of the car and stood staring.

Meg stared too. Looks *and* money, she thought. Recipe for disaster.

Her brain was in a total spin. She'd expected him to slink out before dawn and here he was, smiling at her child. Coming with them to pick a Christmas tree. Playing happy families. Playing puppets, with her heart at the end of the strings.

Only if this went wrong it wasn't going to be one heart that was broken, she thought. It would be two.

'It's just a house, Meg.' Apparently reading her mind, Dino urged her forward. 'I have a friend who is an architect. I persuaded him to sell it to me. He throws himself into a project but once it's completed he's immediately bored and he's ready to start on something else. At the moment he's building something incredible on the coast somewhere with sea views. Come inside.'

The house was built on three floors, one of them below ground level.

'Gym and cinema,' Dino said, intercepting her glance.

'Cinema?' Jamie looked as if he were about to

explode with excitement. 'You have a cinema in your own home? How?'

'I live on my own. I can use the space any way I choose. Come and see.' He led them downstairs and opened a door.

'Mum, look!' Without waiting to be invited, Jamie shot inside and aimed straight for the wall that was lined from end to end with DVDs. 'This is *so* cool. Where are the cartoons? Do you have *Ice Age*? Can I watch in 3D?'

Dino gave him an apologetic look. '*Mi dispiace*, I'm sorry, Jamie.' He cleared his throat. 'I haven't built up my collection of cartoons yet, but I'm planning to do that soon. Perhaps you could give me a list of your favourites.'

Jamie's face fell as he scanned the spines of the DVDs. 'So you only have films with real people?'

'Yes.' Dino smiled at the description. 'Real people.'

Meg stood still, taking in leather and luxury. So he had money. That didn't have to make a difference, did it? The fact that she was talking herself round shocked her and made her realise she was in deeper than she'd ever intended.

She wanted this to work.

Scared, she took a step backwards, as if by leaving the room she could also leave behind the thought. The beat of her pulse quickened.

Jamie didn't share her discomfort. 'It's a shame you don't have any good films.'

'Jamie, this is Dino's house,' Meg forced herself back to the present. 'He's an adult. Why would he have animated films?'

'*You* love *Ice Age* and you're an adult.' Jamie lifted his chin and looked at Dino. 'Have you ever seen it?'

'No.'

'Then how do you know you won't like it?'

'I'm sure I will like it and next time you come, I'll have a section of cartoons, I promise.'

'I could just bring my favourites over here and watch them,' Jamie said helpfully, and Meg gasped.

'Jamie! You can't just—'

'That's an excellent idea.' Dino took the little boy's hand and pulled him across the room. 'There's the projector so you sit on one of those sofas and watch it there—try it for size.'

Jamie sprawled full-length on the sofa. 'It's massive. There's room for me and five friends. Will there be popcorn?'

Dino didn't hesitate. 'Definitely popcorn.'

'This is amazing, isn't it, Mum?'

It was certainly amazingly expensive. Which, try as she may to convince herself otherwise, simply gave him another reason why he wouldn't want to be with a scruff like her for long.

Meg turned away, but not before she'd caught his eye.

'Now what?' His voice was soft. 'If you're looking for more excuses why it won't work, you're wasting your time.'

Suddenly she wanted to ask him why he wanted her. She was complicated, wasn't she? Not just because her head was completely messed up after Hayden, but because she had Jamie. She came as a pair.

A tour of the rest of the house did nothing to calm her fears. The place was sleek, sophisticated and not at all child friendly. Constructed in wood and designed to blend into the forest around it, there were balconies outside the bedrooms, and the huge walls of glass created a feeling of light and space. It was a place to chill out with fine wine and good music. And not a plastic superhero in sight.

'It's a perfect bachelor pad,' Meg said tonelessly, and Dino gave a faint smile.

'It would also make a perfect family home.' His face was inscrutable. 'It's a very adaptable living space. Take a look around. I'm just going to change and then we can buy that Christmas tree.' He disappeared through a set of doors, leaving them alone in the beautiful living area.

'It's like living inside the forest,' Jamie breathed, incredibly impressed as he nosed around the house. 'Wow, this place is *enormous*. Mum, I could use my skateboard inside this room—the floor would be brilliant.'

'Jamie, don't touch anything,' Meg said quickly, grabbing his hand before he could touch a delicate bowl. 'Just—just stand still with your hands by your sides.'

Jamie stood rigidly. 'Why? Why can't I move? Mum, Dino has a swimming pool. He can swim every day. Isn't that awesome?'

'It's awesome.'

Meg moved away, staring out over the forest and the peaks beyond. Her mind, exhausted from worrying and analysing, drifted. Suddenly she saw herself curled up on the deep, comfortable sofa, enjoying the warmth of the fire after a long day in the mountains, gazing at that view. She imagined making love with Dino on the rug, or in the enormous bed she'd spied through one of the open doors. She imagined eating lunch on the balcony on a sunny day, and Jamie playing a game of superheroes in the forest…

'It must be a wonderful house for entertaining. Just think of the parties you could have here.' Catherine Miller looked ecstatic and Meg's own vision of the place suddenly twisted and morphed into something different.

Parties. Her mother was right; this would be a perfect place for entertaining.

It was contemporary, sleek and stylish—like the man. And Dino would entertain, wouldn't he? He was a senior consultant with an extended network of friends and colleagues.

She put out a hand to touch one of the tall, exotic plants and saw her own nails which Ellie had painted quickly the night before. Yes, they were shiny, but they were still short, neat and practical.

The wrong sort of nails. Just as she was the wrong sort of woman.

Furious with herself for tearing everything up before it had even started, Meg whirled round and paced to the other side of the room. Thick rugs covered wooden floorboards in a pale maple and the walls were lined with books. Somehow, the house managed to be cosy and spacious at the same time. Why couldn't she live here? Why couldn't it work? She had to stop doing that thing—what did psychologists call it?—catastrophising or something. Believing that the worst was going to happen.

'I'm having a party here next week.' Dino walked in, a sweater in his hand. 'I'd like you to come. And before you start thinking of excuses, it's just a few friends. People from the hospital. Mountain Rescue Team. Very informal.'

'I'll babysit,' Meg's mother said immediately, but Dino shook his head.

'I'd like you to come. And Jamie. Ellie and Ben are bringing their kids, and Sean and Ally. They can all go downstairs to the den and watch a film. Jamie can choose his favourite.'

'Wow, thanks.' Jamie was buzzing with excitement. 'We can come, can't we, Mum? A Christmas party. Will Santa be here?'

Dino didn't miss a beat. 'He'll be here.'

Meg hesitated. A party with the mountain rescue team and children present wouldn't be formal, would it? No more long dresses and wearing things that she just didn't feel comfortable in. 'I'd like that. Thanks.'

'Good.' He looked at her for a long moment and then smiled. 'So, don't we have a Christmas tree to buy?'

'This one?' Dino winced as another fir tree tried to lacerate his skin. They'd been in the forest for an hour and still they hadn't found a tree that satisfied Meg.

He knew, because he was watching her face all the time. He couldn't stop looking at her. Somehow, after the passion of the night, her hair had curled again and it bounced around her face in golden curls. Her mouth was curved in a permanent smile as she laughed with her child. She looked slightly ruffled, natural, as if she'd just climbed out of bed.

Which she had.

Lust thudded through him. If it hadn't been for the child, he would have tumbled her down onto the floor of the forest and had her gasping his name within seconds.

'Not the right shape. Try that one.' She pointed and Dino lowered the tree he was holding to the ground and picked up the other one, unable to see the difference. They all looked the same to him. A tree was a tree, wasn't it?

'I like that one, Mum. Can we have it?' Jamie jumped on the spot and Dino watched him, envying the child's ability to live in the moment. For a child, it was all about now. Yesterday was gone and tomorrow was too far away to merit a single thought.

He thought about Hayden, and wondered how any man could be stupid enough not to want to be a part of his child's life. People could be selfish, he knew that from his own family experience. And then the child suffered. Except that no one could think Jamie was suffering. Not with Meg as a mother.

'Turn it around—I want to see the back.' Blowing on her hands, she peered at the tree from every angle and eventually pronounced it perfect.

'Are you going to buy a tree, Dino? You're going to need a really big one for your house. Or maybe two trees.' Jamie was glued to his side and Dino was about to answer when he saw the expression on Meg's face.

She was watching Jamie and her heart was in her eyes.

She was so afraid he was going to hurt her child.

'I'm not planning on buying a tree, Jamie.' He focused his attention on the boy. 'I'll be on my own on Christmas Day, so it isn't worth it.'

Jamie looked puzzled. 'How can you be on your own? Where's your family?'

Doing their own thing, as they always had.

'My parents spend Christmas in the States. My sister goes to stay with her husband's family.'

'And they don't invite you?'

Dino wondered how best to deal with the questions without shattering the child's illusions about the world. 'I'm a grown-up, and grown-ups don't always get together with family at Christmas.'

'Yes, they do.' Jamie frowned. 'Grandma is grown up. And she always spends Christmas with us. We all have Christmas together. I think it's mean that they didn't invite you. You can't be on your own. It isn't right, is it, Mummy? You can come to us. Grandma always cooks a turkey and it's massive. We eat it for weeks. You could help.'

Unbelievably touched, it took Dino a moment
to answer. 'That's kind of you, Jamie—'

'So you'll come? Great. That's great, isn't it,
Mum? Dino is going to spend Christmas Day
with us.'

Meg's face was pink. 'Jamie, he may not want
to—our house is really small, and—'

'I'd love to.' Dino watched her face, trying to
read her mind. They hadn't had a chance to talk
about what had happened since she'd bolted from
the bed that morning. About where this was going.
But he knew where he wanted it to go.

All the way.

But he saw the fear in her eyes and knew he
had to take it slowly. 'So, Jamie, do you think I
need my own tree?'

'Of course. Otherwise where do you put your
presents?'

Charmed by the innocence of the conversation,
Dino struggled to find the right answer. 'When
you reach my age, you don't tend to have too
many presents.'

'Why not?' Jamie looked shocked. 'What about
your mum and dad and your sister?'

Dino kept his expression neutral. 'My parents give me money and I choose something for myself. That's what we've always done.'

'What? Even when you were little?' Jamie looked appalled. 'That's awful.' He slipped his hand into Dino's. 'This year, you should try writing to Santa. I know you're big, but you never know. I write to him every year and he *always* comes.'

Finding it difficult to speak, Dino cleared his throat. 'You think he'd come if I wrote to him?'

'Sure. I think so.' Jamie frowned. 'Maybe you ought to tell him that you save a lot of people's lives, just in case he doesn't know that you do that kind of thing. I mean, that's good, isn't it? It's got to be worth something.'

Dino nodded. 'Maybe.' He rubbed his hand over his jaw. 'Where do I post the letter?'

Jamie gave him a puzzled look. 'You put it up the chimney. It just goes.'

'Up the chimney. Right.' He didn't point out that his contemporary fireplace was surrounded by glass. 'Maybe you can help me write it. Have you done yours?'

'Last week.' Jamie tugged at his hat. 'I asked for

a Batmobile toy, and a Nintendo Wii, but I know I won't get both because it's too expensive. I sort of asked him to choose. He knows what would suit you. He's clever like that. What would you ask for?'

Dino looked at Meg, who had wandered off to help her mother choose a tree. 'I have a feeling Santa probably can't give everyone what they want,' he said huskily, and Jamie looked at him and then turned his head.

'You like my mum, don't you? You look at her all the time. And she looks at you, but mostly when she knows you're not looking.'

Digesting that information, Dino dropped down to his haunches so that he was at the same level as the boy. 'I do like your mum, Jamie. I like her a lot.'

Jamie glanced over his shoulder and then leaned forward and whispered, 'If you like my mum, then you need to have a plan, because pretty soon she'll drive you away. That's what she does. She puts men off. I've heard Grandma talking to her. Grandma says she needs to stop shutting people out. I don't quite know what that means, but I know she doesn't kiss anyone. Is that going to be a problem?'

Dino thought about the night before, about Meg stretched out naked underneath him and above him. 'I think I can handle it.'

'The thing that really worries her is that a man might like her and not me.' Jamie fiddled with one of the branches of the tree. 'Not everyone likes kids. My real dad didn't like kids.'

Dino found that his hands had curled into fists. Forcing himself to breathe slowly, he relaxed them. 'Jamie—'

'I used to think it was that he didn't like me, but Mum told me that was wrong. He didn't even wait around for me to be born, so it couldn't have been because he didn't like me, could it?' There was a flicker of uncertainty in his face and Dino put his arms around the boy and dragged him into a hug.

'No, it most definitely could not have been because he didn't like you. Your mum is right, he must just not have wanted kids. If he'd known you there is no way he could have walked away.' Over Jamie's shoulder he saw Meg looking at them. *Saw the anxiety in her eyes.* He gave her a smile and saw her relax slightly. But she kept glancing towards them as she helped her mother choose a tree.

'Mum says it was her fault. Because she's not a girly girl. She says my dad wanted someone who wore a dress all the time and painted her nails pink.' Jamie pulled away. 'Would you want Mum to paint her nails? Because generally she thinks it's a waste of time.'

'I think,' Dino said slowly, 'that I'd want your mum to do whatever she wanted to do. If she wanted pink nails, that would be fine. If she didn't, that would be fine, too.'

'Right, well, that's good. And I know you don't mind that she likes the mountains, because you like them too. Most of the time at weekends we're up in the mountains, training Rambo. And when I'm older she's promised to get me my own puppy to train.' He looked at Dino. 'So what do you think? Do you think you could get to like me? Because I sort of come with my mum, a bit like getting a free toy in the cereal packet.' There was a tremble in his voice and Dino tried to remember another occasion when he'd felt as though his heart was jammed in his throat.

'I already like you, Jamie. I like you a great deal.'

Jamie stood for a moment. 'So the only problem is how to get Mum to stop being scared of you.'

Dino frowned at that interpretation. 'You think she's scared of me?'

'She's scared you might go away, like my dad. Some men do that.' Looking older than his years, Jamie studied the tree. 'I suppose you just have to show her you like her and that you're not going anywhere. But I don't know how you do that. I expect she'll push you away. It's what she always does.'

'I'm not going to let her push me away, Jamie.'

'It will be hard.'

'I don't mind.'

'That's because you're a superhero.' Jamie slid his hand into Dino's. 'Superheroes don't mind when things get tough. That's when they're at their best.'

'I'm not a superhero, Jamie. But I won't let your mum push me away. That's a promise. How old are you again?'

'Seven years and twelve days. I don't know the hours.'

'Well, Jamie…' Dino cleared his throat. 'for seven years and twelve days and I don't know the hours, you are very wise.'

'No worries. Any time you need any advice about girls, just ask.'

CHAPTER SEVEN

'So you didn't make it to the ball.' Ellie gave her a wink and a suggestive smile and Meg gritted her teeth.

'Actually, it wasn't—'

'Honestly, you don't have to explain. I'm thrilled for you.'

'Ellie, we're not—'

'I knew the moment he saw you in that dress, he'd rip it off.'

Remembering exactly what had happened that night, Meg coloured and Ellie punched her gently on the arm and wandered off in the direction of the radiology department, leaving Meg to stew over her relationship with Dino.

Having not thought about sex for a few years, she suddenly couldn't think about anything else. And it didn't help that she seemed to be working every shift with him. Every time she turned round, he was there. And she'd started noticing things she'd never noticed before—like the way he really looked at the patients when he talked to them. The way he paid attention. Listened. The way he kept a cool head no matter what emergency came through the doors of the department. And he was razor sharp. He had a way of sifting through the evidence in front of him and homing in on the important bit that was going to give him the answers. Just watching him work sent a thrill running through her because he was so incredibly clever. She felt a rush of pride and then realised that was ridiculous. What right did she have to feel proud? He wasn't hers, was he? One scorching night wasn't a guarantee of a future. She knew that better than anyone.

As the days passed, Meg started to wonder whether their colleagues were engineering it so that she and Dino worked together as much as possible and decided that they probably were. People thought it was a bit of fun, didn't they? They didn't realise that they were playing games with something that had the potential to explode and wreck a life. *Two lives.*

On the fourth day after the ball, she finally lost it. 'This is meant to be an emergency department,' she snapped at Ellie, 'not a dating agency. Why am I in Resus with Dino for the fourth time this week?'

'Because you make an unbeatable team.' Leaving that ambiguous statement hanging in the air, Ellie scurried off to meet yet another ambulance while Meg was left standing there, wondering why everyone felt they had to interfere. First her mother then Jamie and now her colleagues.

She felt a flash of exasperation, mingled with fear.

Were they all going to pick up the pieces when everything fell apart?

With a growl of frustration, she removed the packaging from a bag of IV fluid and hung it from the drip stand, ready for the next patient unlucky enough to find himself in the resuscitation room.

'Finally, we're on our own.' Dino's voice came from behind her and her breath caught. Awareness came like a blow to the stomach and Meg tried to calm herself before she turned.

'Alone, apart from about a few hundred staff and patients.'

'I've missed you. This has been the longest four days of my life.' He curved his hand around her face, his gaze slumberous and sexy. 'Can I interest you in hot sex on the trolley? Against the wall?'

Her heart skipped and danced. 'Show a little finesse, Dr Zinetti.'

'Finesse? What's that? In case you hadn't noticed, where you're concerned I don't have any.' His smile was at his own expense. 'Remind me.'

It was impossible not to be flattered by the masculine appreciation burning in his eyes. 'You're obviously feeling rather—'

'Desperate?' There was a husky note to his voice. 'You could say that. I want you, Meg. Every minute of every day. And every minute of every night, but let's not go there.'

His words cut her off at the knees. 'I want you, too.' *It was true, so why was she fighting it?* 'Jamie is sleeping over at my mother's tonight because she's taking him on a secret shopping trip tomorrow.'

'Secret?'

'To buy my Christmas present. I'm not supposed to know. So, Dr Hot…' Her heart jerked. 'Do you want to go out tonight? Dinner? Movie?'

'Neither.' He smiled, the stroke of his thumb against her cheek a sensual prelude to the night ahead. 'If I have you all to myself then I want to stay in. All the entertainment I need is right here.' His eyes told her exactly the form the entertainment was going to take and her insides turned to liquid.

'I assumed you'd want to do fancy restaurants and candles and all that sort of thing.'

'If we're only going to have a few hours alone, I don't want to be in the company of others.'

Her protective antennae twitched. 'You find it hard having Jamie around.'

'No. I love having Jamie around.' He lowered his forehead to hers. 'But I also want to rip your clothes off and I don't want to do that in front of your child.' His mouth hovered close to hers and Meg felt suddenly dizzy.

'Right, well, that's…good, because I don't want to shock him.' She leaned in for his kiss but he released her and took a step backwards.

'Better not.'

'No.' She cleared her throat. 'Because it's unprofessional.'

'Actually, it's more that I'm not sure I'll be able to stop. Which I suppose could amount to the same thing. I'll see you tonight, Meg. Don't bother cooking. I'll do something about replenishing the calories we use.'

In the end they didn't bother replenishing calories. Instead, they feasted on each other, making love until the cold winter light slid across the room and sheer exhaustion had her snuggling against him. She tumbled into clouds of warmth, cocooned by the delicious feeling of being close to another human being, and slept deeply.

This time when they woke, there was no rush to move. No subterfuge.

Meg made fresh coffee and plates of scrambled eggs with toast and they ate in bed, talking about everything and nothing.

'What time will Jamie be home?' Dino leaned back against the tangled bedding. 'Should we get dressed?'

'I'm picking him up from my mother's so that there is no repeat of last time.' Meg put the tray on the floor. It came as a shock to realise she could get used to seeing him in her bed. 'We have another hour, at least.'

'A whole hour?' His eyes gleamed with humour. 'How are we going to fill the time?'

It was fun to tease. 'We could go for a run.'

'If it's exercise you want, I have a better idea…'

He rolled her underneath him and his mouth came down on hers just as both their pagers went off.

Cursing in Italian, Dino leaned across and dug his pager out of the pocket of his trousers. 'This had better be something really, really important.' Hair tousled, eyes sexy, he squinted at it. 'A climber has fallen in Devil's Gully. We're closest and they want us to make a start. For the first time in my life I'm thinking of resigning from the team.'

Meg laughed, but she was already out of bed and pulling on her clothes. 'Do we have exact co-ordinates?'

'Yes.' His eyes skimming her body, Dino sighed. 'The guy had better not have taken a stupid risk or I'm going to give him a lecture for ruining my Sunday. I'm not giving this up for anything less than a life-threatening situation.'

'You're not allowed to lecture.' Meg pulled layers over her head and hopped around as she pulled on her socks. 'Don't just lie there staring. Get dressed!'

'If one of us has to abseil into Devil's Gully, it's going to be me. I just want to get that straight right now.' He dressed quickly and she stole a glance, admiring the curves and definition of his muscles.

'Just because you're sleeping with me doesn't mean you can suddenly get ridiculously protective. I can abseil as well as you can. We'll do what needs to be done.'

He fisted his hand in the front of her fleece and pulled her against him. 'I'm protective,' he said huskily, 'that's just the way it is. Get used to it because it isn't going to change.'

'I don't need protecting.'

'Yes, you do.' He claimed her mouth in a brief but devastating kiss. 'Mostly from yourself. You seem to have a talent for smashing anything that comes too close. Come on. We need to move.'

In under three minutes they were in the mountain rescue vehicle. Rambo was in the back, ears pricked, alert.

'What do you mean, I need protecting from myself?' Meg drove and took the fastest route to the car park that was closest to Devil's Gully. 'I don't smash things.'

'Tell me you're not thinking of a thousand reasons why our relationship is never going to work.'

'Not a thousand.' Annoyed that he was so

perceptive, she shifted gear jerkily. 'Even I can't come up with a thousand.'

'That's because I've been keeping you occupied.' He zipped his jacket, wincing as the vehicle hit a bump in the road. 'Keep your eyes on the road. If I have to be driven, the bare minimum I expect is for the driver to look at the road.'

'My eyes are on the road. Don't tell me how to drive.'

'You're so scared of being hurt again you've shut everyone out.' He pushed his hands into gloves, understanding but ignoring her snappiness. 'But you're not shutting me out.'

'Is that a warning?'

'It's just the way it is, so there's no point fighting it. Car park's ahead. If you pull in by the gate, I'll sort out the equipment. And I'm driving home.'

From the car park, it was only a fifteen-minute hike to the top of Devil's Gully, which was just enough time for her to brood on his comments. It wasn't true. She didn't smash anything that came too close. She didn't need protecting from herself. That was a ridiculous thing to say. Her life had been stable over the past seven years, and that was because she'd taken great care to keep it that way. She liked her life.

But she also liked being with him.

And that terrified her.

'I see someone on the path—this must be where they fell.' Dino quickened his pace and they met up with two walkers who were hovering at the top of the gully.

The woman had obviously been crying. 'He was climbing. We were watching him. He was so good. And then he just fell right past his girl-friend. She was screaming but she's stopped now. I think she's paralysed by fear. And he's been dangling from the rope for at least an hour. Any moment now it could snap. But we don't have any equipment. We had no idea what to do so we just called the police.'

Meg stared down into the gully. She saw the girl clinging to the rock face. 'She doesn't look too good.'

Dino was hauling equipment out of his back-pack. 'He's hanging from emergency ropes.'

The woman was shaking. 'At first he was just swinging. We kept thinking the rope would snap. And he smashed into the rock face when he fell. He managed to tie something round his thigh but he's still bleeding. He hasn't moved for the last few minutes.'

'I'm on my way.' Meg had her hand inside her backpack, pulling out her own gear. 'I'll abseil down to him. I'll try and cut a seat in the snow or something for him to sit on while we wait for the helicopter. I know this climb—there are places. There's a ledge just below him.'

'You're not abseiling down.'

'The rock is crumbling here. It's really unstable. That's probably why he fell. I'm lighter than you. It makes sense for me to go.'

'Meg—'

'You're too heavy, Dino. We're wasting time.' She checked the anchors that would hold the rope, looking for signs of corrosion, fractures and movement in the rock. 'If he's been hanging there for a while, the cold is going to be our biggest problem. Once I have him on the ledge, lower me a sleeping bag—something warm, because if he's been hanging there for half an hour, he's going to be cold.'

'You're not going.'

Meg adjusted her harness and jammed a helmet on her head. 'Are you speaking as my lover or as a member of the mountain rescue team?'

A muscle flickered in his cheek. His internal battle was played out across his handsome face.

'Back up your anchors and keep the rope clear of loose rock and sharp edges. Abseil smoothly and directly down the fall line.'

She pulled on gloves and tossed the rope. 'You think I'm doing this for the adrenaline rush?'

He didn't smile. 'Use an autoblock as a back-up to hold the control rope if you let go.'

'I'm not going to let go.' Looking at his face, she felt warmth build inside her. *He cared.* And it felt scarily good. 'I'm tying a French Prusik. Happy? That way, if I decide to live dangerously and let go, I'm not going to fall.' Calm and confident, Meg made five wraps around the rope and then clipped the two ends into the karabiner.

'Get him onto a ledge.' Dino leaned forward and checked her harness. 'Use your radio.'

Meg went over the edge carefully, checking her anchors and the pull of the rope. The first thing she noticed was the bitter cold and the evidence of new snowfall. She cursed as her feet dislodged loose snow and sent it showering over her. She wondered if the weather had contributed to the man's fall. Overhead she heard the clatter of the search-and-rescue helicopter but she forced herself to focus and concentrate on her own descent.

Finally she was next to the injured climber, her cheeks numb with cold. How much colder must he be after being exposed to the weather in this place?

'Hi, there—can you hear me?' She moved her feet across the rock face so that she was next to him, keeping an eye on the rope. 'I'm Meg. I'm with the mountain rescue team.'

His face was a whitish grey, shocked. Blood had stained one leg of his trousers. 'Nick. I'm bleeding. Not good.'

'Well, this is your lucky day because I'm going to do something about that, Nick.'

His lips barely moved. 'C-cold.'

'I know. I'm going to do something about that too.' She glanced at the rock face. Judged the distance. 'Nick, I'm going to move you onto that ledge and see if I can sort out the bleeding. It will be quicker than getting you to the ground.'

'Fiona—my girlfriend...'

'We'll get her down in a minute. You're the priority. Can you move?' Descending half a metre, Meg moved across the rock face and climbed up to the ledge that she knew was under the layers of snow. With her gloved hand she formed a snow shelf. Dino's voice came through the radio and she talked to him briefly, updating him, telling him about the bleeding. Then she carefully helped the injured climber onto the shelf. 'OK, let's see what we're dealing with. Can you undo your trousers? They're an expensive brand—I don't really want to cut them off.'

Nick gave a weak laugh. 'That sounds like an indecent suggestion.'

'Nick, it's minus five.' Meg ripped open a sterile pad and then helped him slide his trousers down to expose the wound. 'Sex isn't exactly the foremost thing on my mind right now. I—' Blood spurted into the air and she slammed the pad down hard on the wound, pressing with her hand 'Right, that's quite a cut you've got there. You must have caught an artery.'

'I gashed it on the rock—it spurted.'

'Still spurting.' The pad was soaked within seconds. Meg increased the pressure.

Nick leaned his head against the rock. 'I tried a tourniquet. Kept releasing it and tightening it but it wasn't easy. Just leave me. Get Fiona.'

'I'm not leaving you.' Her fingers were slippery with the blood. Using her free hand, Meg spoke into her radio. Her own pulse was racing because this wasn't the place to be dealing with a major injury. She had no room to manoeuvre. 'Dino, I'm dealing with a bleeding femoral artery.' She was going to have to apply another tourniquet, up here on a ledge in freezing conditions. What equipment did she have? What could she use? She had another rope in her backpack. Maybe she could cut that—

'Meg.' Dino's voice came over the radio. 'I'm sending down a sleeping bag and Celox. Use Celox to stop the bleeding. Pour it into the wound. Apply pressure for three minutes.'

'Celox. Damn.' Meg blinked. 'I'd forgotten about Celox.'

Nick's eyes opened. 'What's Celox?'

'It stops bleeding by bonding with red blood cells. It gels and produces a clot. It's amazing stuff. Originally developed for battlefield injuries, I think, but now we're using it. Had our first training session last month.' Careful with her balance, Meg took the pack that Dino lowered. Trying to remember what she'd been taught in the last training session, she ripped open the packet and tipped the Celox into the wound. Then she tore open a fresh pad and applied pressure. 'Let's just hope it's as good as they say it is. Apparently it takes less than thirty seconds to clot. It even works in freezing temperatures, which is just as well because that's what we're dealing with here. See?' Relief poured through her as the bleeding ceased. 'It's magic. Otherwise known as a powerful haemostatic agent. You're going to be fine, Nick. We're going to get you out of here and— Nick? Oh, no, don't do this to me—not here...'

'It's all right, Meg, he's still breathing.' Dino spoke from right beside her and she turned with relief, realising that she hadn't even heard his descent.

'What are you doing here? The rock is crumbling and you must have come down far too fast.' Her voice was croaky. 'If I admit that I'm pleased to see you, are you ever going to let me forget it?'

'Probably not.' His hands were over hers, reassuring and strong. 'How's the bleeding?'

'It's stopped. That stuff is like a miracle.'

'You're the miracle, *tesoro*.' Dino took over. He checked Nick and then signalled to the winchman, who was slowly lowered with the stretcher. 'I'm going to get some morphine into him and then we're going to get him onto the stretcher and into the helicopter. It's only a five-minute flight from here.'

The transfer to the helicopter went smoothly. Having discharged his responsibility towards Nick, Dino abseiled down to help Fiona, who was still clinging to the rock face, frozen with fear.

It took him another twenty minutes to calm her sufficiently to be able to help her down the rock face. Finally, when she was safely secured to him, Dino carefully helped her down to the valley floor. Back in the mountain rescue vehicle, they wrapped her in layers to warm her.

'Will Nick be all right?' Her teeth chattering, Fiona huddled deeper inside the coat. 'When he fell, I thought—I thought…'

'He's going to be fine.' Meg cleaned herself up as discreetly as possible, sloshing water over her hands. 'We're taking you to the hospital now, so you can check that out for yourself.'

Ellie met them as they walked into the department. Her eyes sparkled knowingly as she saw Meg and Dino together. 'Enjoying your Sunday?' Without saying anything else, she smiled and slid her arm around Fiona, escorting her to where Nick was being assessed.

'Not subtle, are they?' Meg gritted her teeth. 'I should have got you to drop me off.'

Dino sent her a speculative look. 'I don't see a reason to hide our relationship. Do you?'

Meg shrugged awkwardly. 'Well, we're colleagues. I suppose it's just I don't want everyone knowing. I don't want them all taking bets on how long it is before you go off with some long-legged blonde.'

'You're a long-legged blonde, *amore*.' Dino slid his arm round her waist and pulled her against him. 'And I'm with you.'

Conscious of their surroundings, Meg tried to ignore the sizzle of awareness in her body. 'We're at work.'

'No, we're not. It's our day off.' His mouth was close to hers. 'Stop thinking like that, Meg. Stop thinking this relationship is doomed before it starts.'

'Right. Yes. I'm going to stop.' Meg tried not to think about Hayden. Instead, she found herself thinking about her replacement, the gorgeous Georgina, waiting in the car, her hair smooth and sleek and her mouth a glossy red. *Damn the woman.* 'I'm just going to nip to the staffroom and clean up. Then we can go and pick up Jamie and get your car.'

'Come back to my house for the evening.' Dino

stroked her face with his fingers. 'I'll cook some pasta. We can open a bottle of wine.'

'I have Jamie.'

'He can eat my pasta. And I've bought a selection of DVDs for him.'

'You're kidding.' Meg started to laugh. 'You bought *Ice Age*?'

'I bought every animated film that has been produced in the last ten years, just to be on the safe side. And a mountain of popcorn.'

'Be careful. If you make it too comfortable, we'll move in.'

Something flickered in Dino's eyes and Meg took a step backwards, seriously shaken up by her own thought process. Why had she said that? What was she thinking? 'I—I need to go and clean up. I'll meet you in the car park.' Without giving him time to answer, she shot into the staffroom and into the shower room.

She turned on the hot water and scrubbed her hands, soaping them to remove all traces of the dramatic rescue. Moving in? Since when had sex turned into moving in? Get a grip, Meg. It was all too fast.

She closed her eyes tightly, trying to wipe out

the picture of the three of them curled up on one of Dino's huge, deep sofas, watching a movie.

He liked her, yes. And he liked Jamie. Otherwise why would he have bought an entire collection of movies he was never likely to watch on his own? And he genuinely seemed to find her attractive, even when she was dressed in her walking gear.

So why was she just waiting for it to fall apart?

Reminding herself that Dino wasn't anything like Hayden, Meg dried her hands and opened the door of the shower room. A couple of nurses from the department were making tea and Melissa, the nurse from the observation unit, was in the middle of telling a story about some unfortunate girl whose trousers had split.

'It would help if she ate less chocolate,' she said bitchily, and then broke off as Meg appeared. 'Oh—hi, Meg. Gosh, what have you been doing with your Sunday? You look a total wreck.'

A total wreck.

Angry, Meg pushed her hair away from her face. 'I rescued a man from certain death from a cliff face,' she said coldly. 'What have you been doing with your Sunday, Melissa? Painting your nails?'

Flirting with doctors?

'Apart from working, I've been planning what to wear for Dino Zinetti's Christmas party.' Melissa made herself a herbal tea and declined the offer of a biscuit from one of the other nurses. 'No, thanks. My dress is so-o-o tight there's barely room for me, certainly no room for a biscuit. I want to look like a woman, but not that much of a woman.'

Meg felt sick. Dino had invited Melissa to his party? A few friends, he'd said. Friends from work and members of the mountain rescue team. Since when had Melissa been a friend? He knew it was seeing Melissa that had upset her on the night of the ball.

Nina, one of the other nurses, helped herself to two biscuits. 'So what are you wearing, Meg?'

Meg looked at her blankly. What was she wearing? What sort of a question was that? The party was two days away. Who started thinking about what to wear two days before an event? Dino had told her it was informal. She'd planned to tug open her wardrobe half an hour before she left the house and pick something.

'Meg will wear jeans.' Melissa fished her tea bag out of her mug. 'Meg always wears jeans. And I don't blame you.' She smiled at Meg. 'Jeans are always safe, aren't they? And your legs are quite muscular.'

Muscular?

Meg had an overwhelming temptation to kick one of her muscular legs straight into Melissa's glossy smile.

She wanted to say something witty that would wipe the smirk off the other girl's face, but her mind was completely blank. No words came. Later, she knew, she'd think of something cutting. Later, when it was far too late to say anything, and then she'd spend weeks cursing herself for not thinking of the right thing to say at the right time. But for now there was nothing. So she simply muttered something non-specific and left the room, hating herself for letting them get to her.

Meg will wear jeans. Meg always wears jeans.

What was wrong with that?

What was so clever about pouring yourself into a tight dress that left nothing to the imagination?

Any idiot could plaster themselves with make-up and pout, couldn't they?

Angry and hurt, she stomped towards the back entrance of the department. She'd actually been looking forward to Dino's party, but now she didn't want to go. It was going to be another one of those social events that felt like a competition. *I love your shoes. Oh, that dress is so gorgeous.* A room full of gorgeous Georginas all staring at her and judging.

Meg always wears jeans.

Maybe she'd just tell Dino she wasn't well. But then Jamie would be horribly disappointed and she'd earn herself another lecture from her mother.

Pushing open the doors of the emergency department, Meg paused as the cold air rushed forward to meet her. In the distance she saw the jagged outline of the mountains, topped with snow and sparkling under the winter sun. Just looking at them made her feel instantly better.

Really, she had to get over this. It was just a party. One party. Not a big deal. Nothing worth getting herself into a stew over. She was being pathetic.

Meg breathed in the fresh mountain air and suddenly felt stronger.

Two girls dressed as elves hobbled past her into the building, chatting together. A mother with a pushchair loaded with Christmas shopping negotiated the icy pavement on her way home. Life, Meg thought. A mixture of good and bad. Easy and difficult.

The door swung closed behind her and she saw Dino waiting for her, the collar of his jacket turned up against the cold, his phone in his hand as he scrolled through his messages.

She could ask him why he'd invited Melissa. She could tell him she wasn't coming. Or she could play this another way.

Meg gave a slow smile.

And have some fun.

CHAPTER EIGHT

DINO checked on the caterers and adjusted the volume of the music. People had been arriving for the past hour but there was still no sign of Meg and Jamie.

A tinkle of female laughter scraped against his nerve endings and he clenched his jaw and glanced over his shoulder at Melissa. She stood with her back to the fire, the shimmering light turning her skin-tight black dress transparent. He wondered if she knew her underwear was on display and decided that she did. Melissa did nothing by accident. He knew her type well. Her dress was a message. *I'm yours.*

Except that he didn't want her.

He hadn't invited her, but she'd arrived as part of the group of nurses from the emergency department. Given that the purpose of the party was goodwill, he'd decided to overlook it. But now he was remembering that Melissa had been the reason Meg had run out on him the night of the ball. Had she found out that Melissa intended to show up? Was that why she wasn't here?

If she didn't know, she was going to find out soon enough. And she was going to take one look at Melissa's ultra-short dress and shiny red mouth and turn and run. Again.

Dino felt tension ripple across his shoulders. He'd told her it was casual, hadn't he? He'd set this whole thing up as somewhere comfortable and safe where she could socialise without worrying about what everyone was wearing. He hadn't factored in that it was Christmas and most of the women were looking for an excuse to dress up and flutter their feathers.

Meg was going to arrive in her jeans and feel out of place.

He wondered whether he should call her mobile and warn her. But if he did that, she would definitely freak out and not show.

'Hi, Dino, great party.' One of the consultant radiologists shook his hand firmly and introduced his wife, who was heavily pregnant. 'This is a fantastic place you have here.'

Looking at the throng of people filling his house, Dino gave a humourless smile. Interesting, he thought, how a house could be full of people and yet still feel empty just because of the absence of one person.

Extracting himself from small talk, Dino glanced through the expanse of glass, watching for headlights. People were arriving in a continuous stream, but there was still no sign of Meg.

He was just exchanging a few words with an equipment officer from the mountain rescue team when the room suddenly fell silent. The steady buzz of conversation faded to near silence. Exploring the cause, Dino turned his head and saw Meg standing in the doorway. She was wearing a sparkling blue dress that made Melissa's choice of semi-transparent black look positively dowdy.

Scanning her from the tumble of golden curls to the long, graceful length of her legs, Dino tried to remember how to breathe. What had possessed him to invite all these people when there was only one person who interested him? Why hadn't he just invited her and made it a private party for two? She looked stunning.

And sophisticated.

A pair of killer heels made her legs look impossibly long and the shimmering dress skimmed her athletic physique in a way that suggested rather than shrieked.

'Dino!' Jamie flew across the room, dressed as a superhero, his cape flying behind him. 'Sorry we're late. We were on a mission.'

Dino scooped the boy into his arms, his eyes still on Meg. For a moment she didn't move. She just looked at him. Then she smiled and walked across the room, head held high.

'Dino.'

He'd expected to see insecurity in her eyes but instead he saw fire and fight and felt the tension pulsing from her. Picking up on it, his eyes narrowed in silent question.

Something, or someone, had upset her and she'd come out fighting.

And you didn't have to be a genius to guess who. 'I was beginning to think you weren't coming.'

'Why wouldn't I come?' Her tone was slightly brittle and she helped herself to a glass of orange juice from one of the waiters who were circulating with drinks and canapés. 'This is fantastic. I thought you said it would be just a few friends. Informal.'

'It started out that way but it escalated, and I don't have time to prepare food for this number of people so I thought it was easier to get caterers in. This isn't how I planned it.'

She relaxed slightly and stayed by his side. They chatted about the day and then a couple of members of the mountain rescue team joined them and they all started talking about their latest rescue.

Halfway through the evening 'Santa' appeared with a sack of presents for the children.

As Jamie and the other children leaped around with excitement, Dino watched Meg. Finally she'd relaxed. Drink in hand, she was laughing as Jamie ripped the paper off his present to reveal a large plastic Batman figure.

Dino threw a questioning glance at Meg. 'I know he already has one...'

'It's great. Really thoughtful.' She smiled up at him. 'You can never have too many. I'm trying to work out who is concealed under that Santa suit. It looks like Rob Hamilton from Orthopaedics but he isn't quite that portly. Unless he's hit the mince pies big time.'

'We added some padding to his costume. He has the deepest voice. Not to mention the fact he was one of the few who was prepared to do it. Come on—' He held out his hand. 'Let's dance.'

She hesitated, her cheeks pink. Then she slowly

put her glass down on the table and gave a hesitant smile. 'All right, but I ought to warn you I—'

'Dino!' Melissa bounced over to them, her breasts in danger of making a guest appearance. Grabbing his other hand, she pulled. 'This is my favourite track. Dance with me.'

'I don't think so.' Frowning, Dino extracted his hand but Meg was already backing away, her smile frozen to her face.

'You go ahead. I'm useless at dancing anyway. And I need to see Jamie.'

'Meg—'

'Honestly, dance.' She waved her hand towards the centre of the room. 'I'll catch up with you later.'

Dino reached out to grab her but she melted into the crowd, vanishing in the sea of shimmering dresses that closed in front of him, blocking his path.

She was a complete fool.
Meg stood in the bathroom, staring at herself in the mirror. It was always going to be like this. What had she expected? That she could turn herself into some supermodel overnight? That

putting on a pair of high heels and a sparkling dress would make her feel any different inside?

'Meg?' Dino's voice came through the door. 'Are you in there?'

She froze. 'Give me a minute.'

'I need to talk to you.'

Tugging open the bathroom door, she pinned a smile on her face. 'Hi. Everything all right? The kids haven't discovered the champagne, have they?'

'Why do you do that? You just walked away.' His eyes were very dark and very angry. 'You always walk away when things get tough. You should have stood your ground and fought her.'

'I didn't want to make things awkward for you.'

'Awkward? You think I care about awkward? *Maledezione*, Meg, what do you think is going on here?'

'I think all the women in the room are interested in you—as usual. I think they all spent most of the last week planning what they were going to wear to catch your attention.'

'There is only one woman in the room who interests me. And, no, you're not leaving until we've had this out.' He rested his arm against the wall, trapping her, his eyes stormy. 'If you'd hung around you would have heard me telling Melissa that I'm not interested. That she's wasting her time.'

'It isn't just Melissa.' Meg found that her hands were shaking. 'There will always be another Melissa. That's the sort of man you are.'

His features hardened. 'What's that supposed to mean?'

'You can't help it, Dino. You're super good looking, sexy, rich—basically gorgeous. You only have to smile and women want to rip their clothes off.' Meg gave a hysterical laugh. 'There will always be some woman who wants you. Always some woman trying to knock me down to get to you. Maybe you don't notice Melissa, but sooner or later one of them is going to attract your attention if they try hard enough. And then it's going to be Georgina all over again.'

There was a long silence. 'That was her name?' His voice was harsh. 'The woman he dumped you for?'

Meg shrugged. 'That doesn't matter. What does matter is that the world is full of Georginas. I can't compete. And, actually, I don't want to. I don't want to live my life on a knife edge, wondering whether this is going to be the day you find someone prettier.'

'Have you any idea how insulting that is?' He pulled away from her, his expression black. 'You're implying that I have no control over my own emotions or behaviour, that I'll tangle the sheets with every pretty girl who crosses my path. Is that what you think of me? Is that who you think I am?'

'You're human. You're a man, for God's sake.'

'Yes, I'm a man. A grown man, not some teenage boy who hasn't learned control. Damn it, Meg, I can forgive you for thinking I'm ruled by my libido because that's how it seems whenever I'm with you, but I find it hard to forgive you for thinking I'm so shallow that I'd chase after any woman who throws herself at me. I need more than mindless sex in a relationship. Until you came into my life, I had no trouble at all with the word no. Believe it or not, I'm adult enough to make my own choices. And if a woman comes on to me, it's still my choice, even if her dress is up round her bottom and her boobs are thrust in my face. For your information, Melissa is the type of woman I avoid. I know her type too well.'

'But—'

'No, there are no "buts" on this one Meg.' His tone was hard. 'Maybe you've spent too much time alone with Jamie. You're treating me like a child, assuming that every shiny new toy I see in the store I'm going to want to buy.'

Her heart pounded. 'I'm not treating you like a child.'

'Then trust me, Meg. Trust me to make my own decisions and exercise control. That's what being an adult is all about. I know what I want out of life. And it isn't quick sex with any woman who will put it out there.' A muscle worked in his jaw. 'I wait until I see something good, something special, and when I do I'm not afraid to go for it. Unlike you.'

'I'm not afraid.'

'Yes, you are. You're terrified of being hurt again the way Hayden hurt you, and I understand that. But we can't have a proper relationship if I'm having to look over my shoulder all the time, checking there are no pretty girls in the vicinity in case you're about to go into meltdown. I can't live like that. There has to be trust, Meg.'

He didn't understand. He had absolutely no

idea. Meg felt tears prick her eyes. 'I can't live like that either. I can't live my life wondering whether today is going to be the day you tell me I'm not the woman you want to be with. Wondering whether this is going to be the day you walk out and go off with the more glamorous model waiting in the wings. I sometimes wonder if you even realise how sexy you are. You walk into a room and there isn't a woman who doesn't look at you! And I don't think I can stand by and watch a never-ending string of glamorous woman dress up and try and attract you away from me. And maybe that's defeatist, but it's the way it is. I don't want to live my life with a knot of anxiety in my stomach. It isn't fair on me and it isn't fair on Jamie. And it isn't fair on you because I don't think I can change. And I know this is just me being stupid. I know that. But I can't change the way I think.' Her breathing was shallow.

'You're right that I'm afraid. I admit it, I'm terrified! Terrified that I'll put Jamie through what I went through. Terrified that I'll have to answer another load of questions about why another man left him. I just don't want to risk that. I can't.' She waited for him to give a sympathetic nod or acknowledge in some way that he understood what she was feeling.

Instead, he pulled away from her, his eyes cold. 'If you think I'd hurt your son, you don't know me at all.'

'It isn't about not knowing you. It's about reality.' She struggled to make him understand. 'Relationships break up every single day.'

'Not all of them. Have you thought about that, Meg? Some relationships actually work out. The good ones.'

'But how do you know?' Her voice was a whisper. 'If I get this wrong, Jamie gets hurt. I can't do that to him.' And she couldn't do it to herself.

'So you'll trust me with your life on the end of a rope, but you won't trust me with your heart.' His tone was raw. 'Is that right?'

Meg stared at him.

She wanted to tell him that she trusted him. But the words couldn't break free from the cold ball of terror inside her.

Dino watched her for a long moment. Waited. And then turned and walked away, leaving her standing alone, drowning in a sea of her own fears.

* * *

Meg drove home, Jamie asleep in the back of the car.

Twice she had to stop because she was crying so hard and she couldn't see the road. She'd blown it. She'd totally blown it. Ruined everything.

As she drove through the town on the way to her house, she saw crowds of people pouring out of restaurants and bars after Christmas parties. They wore silly hats and tinsel and clutched presents. They were all laughing and chatting and they seemed so *normal*. Whereas she—she was so messed up she didn't have a clue how to fix herself.

Why couldn't she just have said she trusted him? Even if it all went wrong, could it honestly feel any worse than this?

She could have carried on, couldn't she, hoping that he kept looking at her and no one else?

But she was exhausted with being on her guard and watching for competition. Wiping the smile off Melissa's face should have been fun, but she'd felt nothing except a bone-deep tiredness.

Flicking her indicator, she took the road that led out of the town towards the lake. Was Dino with her now? Had he turned to her for consolation?

As she drove down the lane that led to her

house, the moonlight reflected off the snow and the mountains stood out clearly. It was midnight, but she could see the contour of every peak and she could name them. She'd climbed most of them with Dino by her side. He was right when he'd said she trusted him with her life. She did. Out here, in her world. In the place that mattered to her, she trusted him.

Here, she could be herself. Here, it didn't matter who designed your handbag or whether your dress was 'last season'. Here, it was more important to know whether there might be a new snowfall overnight, bringing more risks to walkers in the morning. Here, you had to be able to recognise wind slab and know how to use an ice axe. Here, she was comfortable.

Functioning on automatic, Meg pulled up outside the cottage and gently lifted Jamie out of the back seat of the car. He snuggled against her, his arms tight around her neck. For a moment she held him against her, taking comfort from the feel of his warm, solid body crushed against hers. He was her world. Her whole world.

'It was a lovely party, Mummy.' His voice was sleepy. 'Popcorn. *Ice Age*. And tomorrow is Christmas Eve. I love Christmas Eve because Christmas is still to come and it's so exciting.'

Struggling to find even a glimmer of excitement inside herself, Meg picked her way through the fresh snow. 'What about Christmas Day? Don't you like that?'

'Christmas Day is the best. I can't wait to see Dino again.'

Meg held him tightly with one arm and pushed her key in the door. Looking at the mistletoe, she lifted her hand and pulled it off the door. No more mistletoe. No more dreams and delusions. Flinging it onto the snow, she took a deep breath. 'He's not coming, Jamie.' Her voice was gruff. 'He can't make it for Christmas Day. I'm sorry.' She carried him into the house and Jamie lifted his head groggily. Still sleepy, he focused on her face.

'He *is* coming. He promised.'

'No. No, he's not. It's not his fault.' Her voice cracked. 'It's my fault. It's all my fault.'

'He said he was coming!' Fully awake now, Jamie wriggled out of her arms. 'He promised! He promised he wouldn't let you push him away! He promised he wouldn't let that happen. *He promised!*'

'Jamie…' Shocked, Meg held out her arms to him but he backed away, tears pouring down his cheeks.

'He promised. Just leave me alone! I hate you and I hate Dino! I thought he was a superhero but he isn't. He isn't. He's just a man and I hate him.' Sobs tearing his little chest, Jamie ran upstairs to his bedroom and slammed the door.

Meg closed the front door and leaned her head against the wood, beating herself up for choosing to tell him now and not wait until the morning when he'd slept and was better able to cope with disappointment. She'd told him, she realised numbly, because she'd needed to talk to someone. But that shouldn't have been Jamie, should it? He was a child.

She was crying too, hot tears smudging the mascara she'd applied so carefully only a few hours earlier. She wanted to go after Jamie, but she knew he needed a few minutes to calm down by himself.

In a minute she'd go upstairs and tuck him in. Read to him. Stories where a superhero always stepped in when life got hard.

If only…

She needed to explain to him that none of this was Dino's fault. It was her, wasn't it?

She was a coward.

She'd fallen over once, hurt herself badly, and now she was afraid to run again. Her mother was right—hanging from a rock face from a thin rope wasn't brave because she wasn't afraid of that. Brave was when you did something that terrified you. Tonight, she'd stared her biggest fear in the face. And she'd turned and run.

'Jamie is quiet, considering it's Christmas Eve.' Meg's mother sprinkled icing sugar over the Christmas cake to look like snow. Outside, the sun shone on the snow crystals, adding sparkle and light. 'Is he just tired or has something happened?'

'Do you really need to ask? Don't put any more sugar on that, Mum, or our teeth will fall out.'

'I assume this has something to do with Dino?'

'That's right. I messed it up. As always.' Her tone brittle, Meg emptied cranberries into a saucepan. 'How much water do I add to these?'

'Just a tablespoon. And the zest of an orange. So are you going to fix it?'

'Dino broke up with me, Mum.'

She frowned. 'Really? That surprises me. He doesn't strike me as the sort who walks away.'

'No, that's usually my role.'

'Did he say why?'

'He was angry that I wouldn't trust him. Angry that I was worried he might go off with someone.' She swallowed. 'He said he couldn't live like that.'

'Waiting for you to destroy something good? I don't blame him. You're enough to give the most patient man an ulcer. Don't stir those so hard— they're nicer when they're still whole. I like bite and texture.'

Meg stopped stirring. Her eyes were gritty from lack of sleep and her head ached. But none of that came close to the agony that burned inside her. 'I feel…h-horrible. Miserable. And so, so guilty about Jamie. He wanted it to work out so badly. And the crazy thing is I wanted that too. I wanted us to be a family. I wanted that.' Her voice cracked. 'What have I done, Mum?'

Her mother made a distressed sound and crossed the kitchen. 'Oh, sweetheart…' She folded Meg into her arms and held her tightly, crooning as she had when Meg had been a small child. 'You haven't done anything. You're just sorting out your thoughts and the way you feel and that takes time. You're too hard on yourself.'

Meg sobbed into her mother's shoulder, unravelling in the safe cocoon of warmth and love. 'No, I've wrecked everything and it could have been good because Dino is just gorgeous, not to mention clever, and he's so lovely with Jamie and he's incredible in bed.' She sniffed. 'Sorry—I'm so sorry.'

'Don't apologise.' Her mother stroked her hair away from her face. 'I'm so proud of you and everything you've done. And now you're going to listen to me. You've done a fantastic job with Jamie. You're a wonderful mother, but there are times when you need to put yourself first and this is one of them. Stop worrying about Jamie and think about yourself. Why do you think you're so scared, Meg?'

'Apart from the fact that I'm a crackpot?' Meg found a tissue and blew her nose. 'Because of Hayden, I suppose.'

'You were young and vulnerable when you met Hayden. A girl, not a woman. You were attracted by surface sparkle and you didn't notice the lack of depth.' Her mother urged her gently to a chair.

'If Hayden walked through that door now, what would you do?'

'Kick him out again. I know he wasn't right for me, Mum. I know it would never have lasted, but knowing that doesn't help.'

'When Hayden left you were young, you were pregnant, you were alone. But you survived. And you would survive again. People do.' Her mother's face was sad and Meg leaned forward and hugged her, feeling horribly selfish.

'When we lost Dad I was worried you wouldn't survive. I was worried you wouldn't want to live your life without him.'

'I learned to live a different life.' Her mother's voice was quiet. 'There isn't a day when I don't miss your father and I'd be lying if I said it never hurts, but that doesn't mean I'm not happy. Loving and being loved is the greatest gift of all. It's what life is all about, and that's what I want to see in your life. I don't want to see you turning love away because you're afraid of what will happen if you lose it. If you do that, you've already lost.'

'Love? Who said anything about love?' Meg stared, her heart pumping hard. 'I'm not— I don't…' She gulped. 'Oh…'

'Why do you think you're so very scared?' Her

mother's voice was gentle. 'Why does it matter so much?'

Meg sucked in a breath. 'Because I love him. I love him so much it's like this huge glowing thing inside me. When I'm with him I feel as though I'm a light that's suddenly switched on. I love him, *I love him*, but I couldn't say it, and now—now—'

'That's why you're scared. Not because of Hayden or that stupid Georgina girl. But because this time you really care and when we really care it makes us vulnerable.'

Meg pressed her hand to her chest and looked at her mother. 'What do I do? Tell me what to do.'

Her mother smiled, love in her eyes. 'I think you already know the answer to that one.'

'I think I need to find out if he loves me. But he's never said—what if he doesn't?'

'He's human too. He's not going to put it all out there unless he thinks there's a chance, and you've been pushing him away from day one. How many months have you worked together?'

'Eight? Nine?' Her brain was a mess. 'I don't know.'

'And he's been biding his time.'

'He flirted with everyone. He only asked me out recently. Why?'

Her mother smiled and stood up. 'Why don't you ask him?'

'Right now?' Meg found it difficult to breathe. 'Wh-what are you going to do?'

'Stay with your son.' Her voice calm, Catherine opened the fridge. 'Go. You have a whole life to live, Meg. And I have a turkey to stuff.'

CHAPTER NINE

THE house looked empty. Quiet after the noise of the night before, the huge windows reflecting the green of the forest and the bright winter sunshine.

There was no sign of life.

Meg left her car and stood for a moment, breathing in the scent of pine. The whole place smelt like Christmas.

They could live here, she thought. They could make a life together. Be a family.

If that was what he wanted. If she wasn't too late.

Walking towards the front door, she wondered if he'd seen her arrive. No, because he wouldn't ignore her, would he? She refused to be that paranoid. If he'd seen her arrive, he would have answered the door. He wasn't the sort to run and hide in the basement.

Her hand shook as she pressed the bell.

If her mother was wrong then she was about to

make a total fool of herself. She was about to put her heart out there—everything she felt. She was giving him the chance to squash it.

Except that he wasn't answering.

Which meant he obviously wasn't sitting around brooding or getting blind drunk.

He'd gone out. Unless—unless he was inside and he already had company.

Feeling her courage drain away, Meg bit her lip, realising that the party had probably gone on long after she'd left. As far as he was concerned, their relationship was over. What was to stop him finding someone else?

The cold seeped through her jumper but Meg barely noticed.

She'd ruined everything. She should have been brave.

But she hadn't.

And now she'd lost him.

It was over.

'Mummy, wake up! He's been! Can I open my stocking in your bed?' Without waiting for an invitation, Jamie dragged his lumpy, bumpy stocking into the bed and Meg struggled to wake up.

She glanced at the clock and realised she'd been asleep for less than two hours.

'It's still only seven o'clock, Jamie, so don't make too much noise. Grandma is asleep and she doesn't want to be woken up this early.'

'Do you need coffee or something?' Jamie peered at her. 'You look funny.'

'I just haven't quite woken up yet.' Meg sat up and tried to shake off the sleep. 'But I'm working on it. Right. What's in this stocking?' Even half-asleep and broken-hearted, she enjoyed watching him dig the presents out of the stocking and rip off the paper. They were just small things, but from the look on his face he might have been given the world. Watching his delight at discovering a Batman torch that had cost her less than a cup of coffee, she felt a rush of pride and gratitude. He was such a sweet-natured boy. So undemanding compared to so many of the other children she saw, who were only interested in the label or the 'next big thing'.

'This is so cool.' He lay on his back on her bed, flashing the torch at the ceiling. 'Watch, Mum. The beam is the shape of a bat.'

'I'm watching.'

'Isn't Santa clever, Mum? He knows exactly what I want.'

Meg swallowed. The one thing he really wanted she hadn't been able to give him.

She'd failed at that.

Racked with maternal guilt, she wrapped her child in her arms and hugged him tightly. 'I love you.'

'I love you, too. Can I give you my present to you now?'

'You don't want to wait for Grandma?'

'Grandma helped me choose. Please? I want to see your face when you open it. You're going to be so thrilled.'

His enthusiasm was so infectious that Meg grinned. 'Go on, then.'

'Are you excited?'

'I'm excited.'

Jamie flew off the bed and reappeared moments later with a parcel. The wrapping paper was falling off and the whole thing was loosely bound together with metres of sticky tape. 'I wrapped it myself.'

'I see that. Good job.' Meg handled it carefully, trying to extract her fingers from all the sticky tape. 'Wow. What is it?' She eased the present out of the wrapping and smiled. 'Mrs Incredible pyjamas. How perfect.' She swallowed. No matter what she did, however many mistakes she made, to him she was still Mrs Incredible.

Meg studied the pyjamas through a mist of tears.

'They're red. And when you put them on, you look exactly like Mrs Incredible.' Jamie beamed at her. 'Super-Mum, that's you. I chose them myself. Do you like them?'

'I love them.' Her voice was thickened. 'They're the nicest thing anyone has ever given me.'

'So are you going to put them on?'

'Absolutely. Right away. I'll wear them for breakfast.' Glad of an excuse to leave the room and get herself under control, Meg picked up the pyjamas and walked to the bathroom.

Jamie called after her. 'While you're getting changed, I'll just eat the chocolate from my stocking.'

'Before breakfast?' Meg brushed the tears from her cheeks. 'Yes, why not? Enjoy. Don't get chocolate on my bed.'

They'd be all right, she told herself. They'd get through. But it was an effort to put on the pyjamas and an effort to drag herself down to breakfast.

Her mother had switched on the Christmas tree lights and Meg's living room looked cosy and festive.

After Jamie had opened his other present from her, a Nintendo Wii that she'd saved up to buy him, she left him playing and found her mother in the kitchen.

'He seems happy.'

'Of course he's happy. He's a child. Children are resilient. More resilient than we give them credit for. I've made a pot of coffee. Strong coffee.' Her mother handed her a mug. 'You look as though you need it, Mrs Incredible.'

'Thanks.' Meg looked down at herself. 'I don't deserve these. He should have bought me Mrs Make a Mess of Everything. They didn't have a pair of those in the store, did they?'

'Mum! Grandma!' Jamie tore through the house, his eyes shining. 'Look outside! I thought the Wii was the best present ever—oh, Mummy, thank you, thank you.' Still in his Batman pyjamas, he dragged open the door and ran into the snow, Rambo barking at his heels.

'Wh-what? Jamie, put a coat on!' Appalled, Meg followed him, shivering in her own thin pyjamas. 'It's *freezing* out here! What do you think you're…?' She stopped, her jaw dropping as she saw the sleek Batmobile crouched on her front lawn. It was child-size, perfect for a boy of Jamie's age. 'What? What is going on?'

'Oh, Mummy, thank you, thank you.' Jamie was almost incoherent with excitement as he slid into the driver's seat. 'How does it work?'

'Jamie I have no idea. I didn't— It isn't from me.'

'It's from me. I hope you don't mind.' Dino walked across the snow towards her, his black hair gleaming under the sun.

Meg stood still, shocked into silence by his unexpected appearance. 'Dino…'

'Merry Christmas, Mrs Incredible.'

Suddenly remembering that she was still wearing Jamie's Christmas present, Meg tugged at her pyjamas self-consciously. Great. If she'd had to meet Dino straight from bed, she would have chosen to be wearing some shimmering slip of silk. Not novelty pyjamas. 'I didn't expect to see you. What are you doing here?'

'You invited me to spend Christmas Day with you.' He slid his hand under her face and held her gaze for a moment before turning back to Jamie. 'It works on the snow. It will pretty much drive anywhere, but we can work out the best places together. Come inside and put on a coat and then we can try it out properly.'

Jamie was completely still, his eyes huge and wary as he stared at Dino. 'You left.' His tone was accusing. 'You said you wouldn't let her push you away, but you did.'

'No, I didn't. Sometimes girls need a bit of space to think things through and I was giving her space.' Dino dropped into a crouch so that he was at eye level with the little boy. 'I didn't let her push me away, although she tried pretty hard. That's why I'm here now. I came back.'

Jamie's fists clenched on the steering-wheel. 'Are you going to go away again?'

'Never.'

'What if she tries to make you?'

'She won't. Not when I've had a chance to talk to her properly.' Dino stood up and held out his arms to the child. 'I'm glad you like the present, but you need to be wearing a few more layers before you play in it or you'll give your mum a reason to be angry with me. Let's go inside and come out again when you're dressed.'

As Jamie sprang into Dino's arms, Meg discovered she was shivering, but whether it was the cold or the fact that Dino was there, she didn't know.

What did he mean when he said he wouldn't go away again?

Her mind spiralled round and round and it was only when she was back in the warmth of the living room that she realised that Jamie and her mother had left her alone with Dino.

'There are things I need to say to you.' Uncharacteristically hesitant, he shrugged off his coat and threw it onto the sofa. 'Things I probably should have said to you a long time ago.'

'There are things I need to say to you, too. I went over to your house. I wanted to see you. To talk to you.'

'You did? I wish I'd been there and then perhaps both of us wouldn't have suffered another sleepless night. I went for a walk. I needed to think.' Lifting his hand, he brushed the dark shadows under her eyes with his fingers. 'I owe you an apology for what I said the other night. I was way out of line.'

'You weren't out of line. Everything you said was true. I do sabotage every relationship. It is a ridiculous way to live. I am a terrible coward. All those things are true.'

'I was too hard on you, but I was offended that you didn't trust me. Offended that you'd think I was the sort of person who would go after Melissa just because she likes to walk around with most of her body on show. As if I didn't have a brain or a mind of my own.'

'Dino—'

'And then I realised that the reason you didn't feel secure in our relationship is because I've never given you any reason to feel secure. I've been holding back telling you how I feel because I didn't want to scare you off. And that's stopped you understanding why our relationship is going to work. I love you, Meg.' He cupped her face in his hands and stared into her eyes. 'I love everything about you. And I'm not talking about a sparkling blue dress or a pair of high heels. I'm talking about what's inside you. I love your energy and your spirit. I love the way you won't hesitate to risk your life to save an injured child, the way you'll make split-second decisions when it's life and death but haven't got any confidence to choose a lipstick.'

Meg's knees were shaking. 'I suppose I'm just basically weird.'

'Gorgeous.'

'I'm messed up.'

'Human. And very beautiful.'

Her heart skipped and danced. 'You can't possibly think that.'

'Meg, I grew up in a family that was completely obsessed with appearance and material things. I came to England to escape from the oppressive expectations of my family. Our home was like a museum and my mother was like one of those mannequins that you see at the waxworks. Beautifully dressed but with no heart or soul. In my entire childhood I don't ever remember her hugging me. Not once. Yes, her nails were perfect and I never once saw her without lipstick, but she wasn't a real person to me. You're a flesh-and-blood woman with feelings and emotions, and you let it all hang out there. You're so open and honest, so warm and emotional. You don't do anything by halves and I love that. I love you, *tesoro*. Every single thing about you. I've waited for you all my life.'

Her heart clenched and she hardly dare breathe in case she disturbed the moment. 'Truly? That's how you feel?'

'I thought it was obvious.'

'No.' She forced the word out. 'No, it wasn't obvious to me.'

'Then perhaps you weren't looking.'

'I just didn't think— I'm not…' She gave a helpless shrug. 'You're so good-looking.'

'I'm glad you think so.' His smile was slow and sexy. 'Say that to me again later when I'm in a position to do something about it, Mrs Incredible.'

'I don't deserve to be wearing these.' Meg bit her lip. 'I'm not Mrs Incredible.'

'To your son, you are. And to me.' He lowered his mouth to hers and kissed her gently. 'I just didn't realise Mrs Incredible was this sexy.'

She laughed against his lips. 'Oh please—sexy? It's hardly sophisticated lingerie, is it?'

'No—' his eyes were amused '—which just goes to prove my point. It isn't what you're wearing that interests me. Although just for the record I think the pyjamas are cute. I'm assuming they were Jamie's choice.' He pulled her against him, leaving her in no doubt about the way he felt. 'If you can do this to me wearing Mrs Incredible pyjamas, I don't even want to think what you can do to me in sophisticated lingerie.'

She threw herself against his chest, her sob of happiness muffled against his chest. 'I was so scared of getting involved with you. Right from the first day you strolled into the department with your lopsided Italian smile and your fancy car and your incredible body, I avoided you like measles.'

'I know. It took me a long time to win you round. You're a hard nut to crack, Meg Miller.'

'Do you know why I was so afraid?' Meg sniffed and lifted her head to look at him. 'Because I love you so much. If I lost you it would really matter.'

'I know you love me. I worked that out during my long walk yesterday. And you're not going to lose me, *tesoro*. Not now, not ever.'

'Other women look at you all the time. Wherever we go, they look at you.'

'If other women look at me, that's their problem.' He stroked her hair away from her face. 'I make my own choices. And I choose you.'

Meg couldn't breathe. 'Dino—'

'Let me finish. You told me you don't want to spend each day wondering whether this will be the day when I tell you I don't want to be with you any more. Well, you're not going to be wondering that, Meg, because each day I'm going to be telling you how much I love you and how much you mean to me. You're not going to be wondering, *amore*, because you're going to *know*. You're going to know I love you.'

Meg made a sound somewhere between a laugh and a sob and he brought his mouth down on hers in a possessive kiss.

'Grandma, they're kissing! You were right about the mistletoe. It's magic.' Jamie's voice came from the doorway and both of them jerked backwards. 'I want to play in my car. Dino, are you ready?'

'*Sì*, yes.' His voice was rough and his eyes were still on Meg, 'I'm ready, but first I have a present for your mother.'

'A present?' Jamie leaped onto the sofa, his Batman cape flying. 'Can I watch while she opens it? Grandma!' he yelled at the top of his voice. 'Dino is giving Mum her present. What is it? Do you need any help opening it, Mum?'

'I don't know, I…' Bemused, Meg stood in the middle of the room and gasped as Dino pulled a small box out of his pocket. 'Oh.'

Jamie's face fell and he looked at her sympathetically. 'It's really small, but it's the thought that counts, Mum.'

Fingers shaking, Meg undid the silver wrapping paper. A shower of tiny silver stars fell to the floor and she stared down at the black box with her heart bursting out of her chest.

Dino removed it from her hand and opened it. A huge diamond solitaire sparkled against midnight-blue velvet.

'Dino...' Meg whispered his name, her feelings overflowing.

'Gosh!' Jamie stood on tiptoe and peered at the box. 'It's a ring. Mum doesn't really wear jewellery. She doesn't wear rings, Dino.'

'She'll wear this one. This one says she's mine.' He took her hand in his and slid the ring onto the third finger of her left hand. 'Marry me, Meg. I want to be with you and Jamie for ever.'

Tears scalded the back of her throat. 'I don't know what to say.'

'You say yes.'

She smiled through her tears. 'Yes—oh, yes—of course, yes.'

Jamie stared up at them, his eyes bright with tears. 'For ever? You mean Dino is never going away again?'

'I promised you I wouldn't.' Dino scooped him into his arms. 'I promised you I wouldn't let her push me away. I never will.'

Jamie buried his face in Dino's neck, his small

hands clinging. 'Mine. You're going to be all mine. My very own superhero.'

'No, Jamie.' Dino's voice was husky as he held the child. 'I'm not your very own superhero. I'm going to be your dad. We're going to be a family.'

Meg closed her eyes, breathing in happiness and thinking of the future.

A family. Her family. A million moments, lived together.

Mistletoe and magic.

'Talking of families…' Her mother's voice came from the doorway. 'If you'd all like to come to the table, we have a turkey to eat.'

MEDICAL™

Large Print

Titles for the next six months...

June

ST PIRAN'S: THE WEDDING OF THE YEAR	Caroline Anderson
ST PIRAN'S: RESCUING PREGNANT CINDERELLA	Carol Marinelli
A CHRISTMAS KNIGHT	Kate Hardy
THE NURSE WHO SAVED CHRISTMAS	Janice Lynn
THE MIDWIFE'S CHRISTMAS MIRACLE	Jennifer Taylor
THE DOCTOR'S SOCIETY SWEETHEART	Lucy Clark

July

SHEIKH, CHILDREN'S DOCTOR...HUSBAND	Meredith Webber
SIX-WEEK MARRIAGE MIRACLE	Jessica Matthews
RESCUED BY THE DREAMY DOC	Amy Andrews
NAVY OFFICER TO FAMILY MAN	Emily Forbes
ST PIRAN'S: ITALIAN SURGEON, FORBIDDEN BRIDE	Margaret McDonagh
THE BABY WHO STOLE THE DOCTOR'S HEART	Dianne Drake

August

CEDAR BLUFF'S MOST ELIGIBLE BACHELOR	Laura Iding
DOCTOR: DIAMOND IN THE ROUGH	Lucy Clark
BECOMING DR BELLINI'S BRIDE	Joanna Neil
MIDWIFE, MOTHER...ITALIAN'S WIFE	Fiona McArthur
ST PIRAN'S: DAREDEVIL, DOCTOR...DAD!	Anne Fraser
SINGLE DAD'S TRIPLE TROUBLE	Fiona Lowe

MEDICAL™

Large Print

September

SUMMER SEASIDE WEDDING	Abigail Gordon
REUNITED: A MIRACLE MARRIAGE	Judy Campbell
THE MAN WITH THE LOCKED AWAY HEART	Melanie Milburne
SOCIALITE...OR NURSE IN A MILLION?	Molly Evans
ST PIRAN'S: THE BROODING HEART SURGEON	Alison Roberts
PLAYBOY DOCTOR TO DOTING DAD	Sue MacKay

October

TAMING DR TEMPEST	Meredith Webber
THE DOCTOR AND THE DEBUTANTE	Anne Fraser
THE HONOURABLE MAVERICK	Alison Roberts
THE UNSUNG HERO	Alison Roberts
ST PIRAN'S: THE FIREMAN AND NURSE LOVEDAY	Kate Hardy
FROM BROODING BOSS TO ADORING DAD	Dianne Drake

November

HER LITTLE SECRET	Carol Marinelli
THE DOCTOR'S DAMSEL IN DISTRESS	Janice Lynn
THE TAMING OF DR ALEX DRAYCOTT	Joanna Neil
THE MAN BEHIND THE BADGE	Sharon Archer
ST PIRAN'S: TINY MIRACLE TWINS	Maggie Kingsley
MAVERICK IN THE ER	Jessica Matthews